my ultimate sister disaster

Also by Jane Mendle

Better Off Famous?
Kissing in Technicolor

my ultimate sister disaster

Jane Mendle

ST. MARTIN'S GRIFFIN NEW YORK

This is a work of fiction. All of the characters, organizations, and events portrayed in this novel are either products of the author's imagination or are used fictitiously.

Printed in the United States of America. For information, address St. Martin's Press, 175 Fifth Avenue, New York, N.Y. 10010.

www.stmartins.com

Library of Congress Cataloging-in-Publication Data

Mendle, Jane.
My ultimate sister disaster / Jane Mendle. — 1st ed.
p. cm.
Summary: Fourteen-year-old Franny barely copes with high school, having a crush on the school newspaper's editor, and practically being parentless, and then her sister, a promising ballerina, breaks her leg and complicates everything.
ISBN 978-0-312-36904-0
[1. Sisters—Fiction. 2. Family life—New York (State)—New York—Fiction. 3. Journalism—Fiction. 4. Ballet dancers—Fiction. 5. High schools—Fiction. 6. Schools—Fiction. 7. New York (N. Y.)—Fiction.] I. Title.
PZ7.M52538My 2010
[Fic]—dc22

2009046751

First Edition: June 2010

10 9 8 7 6 5 4 3 2 1

For my parents—who are nothing like Franny and Zooey's parents—but who will nevertheless worry that they are

my ultimate sister disaster

chapter 1

It's not like I'm complaining. Really. Because I guess my life could be a whole lot worse than it really is. So all I'm going to say is this: If I were to wander into an old dusty junk shop somewhere in Greenwich Village and uncover a beat-up brass lamp stuffed in a corner that the owner would sell to me with a knowing twinkle in his eye, and later I were somehow to run my hand across the surface of the lamp and this magical genie appeared in a poof of smoke . . .

Well, I couldn't wish for anything.

Not because I don't have wishes. I mean, obviously there are tons and tons of things that I want. It's just that there is absolutely no way I could ask this genie-who-would-never-exist-anyway for the stuff that I want. Because if he really were a genie and my wishes were to come true, it would be a major problem. Because there's no way that I could get the things that I want without unleashing a flood of other problems so monumental that it might actually cause the earth to whirl on its axis.

You probably think I'm exaggerating. You probably think I'm one of those teenagers who's suffering from terrible self-esteem even though I'm tall and gorgeous and have Pantene-commercial hair and make straight A's and am about to be elected homecoming queen and teachers say I'm the most sensitive student they've ever had.

That's really not the case. Here's why.

Wish number 1: I would like to run blissfully into the sunset with River McGee or, at the very least, for the boy to notice my existence. I have been in high school for exactly thirty-nine days now, and it would not be an exaggeration to say that I have been obsessed with River McGee for thirty-eight of them. The boy is as organically perfect as his name: cinnamon-colored hair, clove-colored eyes, a journalistic mind as piercingly quick as the actual current in an actual river.

I get to see a lot of River McGee because he is the editor of our school newspaper, the *Suffragette Flyer*, and I am a staff peon. Given that I spend so much time with River, you'd think it wouldn't be such a production for those darkly rich eyes to alight on me. But remember the teen that I'm not? The tall, gorgeous one with the Pantene-commercial hair? That's River's girlfriend, Brianna Bronstein. And the one time that I actually attempted to sit at the long, scarred table with the other newspaper staffers, she rolled her eyes dramatically beneath her well-mascara-ed lashes and sighed.

"Ferny?" she asked coolly.

"Franny," I corrected her.

"Uh-huh," she continued. "That's actually *my* seat you're sitting in. I'm sure you didn't mean to intrude." She waited with her little button nose wrinkled in phony puzzlement as I gathered my stuff together and slunk off to the only chair left available, which happened to be in the very dark back corner of the room, where no one—River included—would ever notice me unless I did something radically attention-provoking and un-Frannyish, like tap-dancing in a negligee. Under her breath, Brianna muttered, "First-years." (Note: The term is *first-years*, and never fresh*men*, at the Elizabeth Cady Stanton School. Please.)

At any rate, let's think about this for a second. Brianna Bronstein shot daggers at me because I accidentally sat in her chair. Can you imagine what the girl might do if I actually deserved her wrath? Like, say, by having her boyfriend gaze at me with that same tenderness he typically reserves for her?

I would seriously fear for my life. So, yeah. Wish number 1 evaporates in a puff of smoke for the simple reason that I would rather not have to deal with reattaching my brain stem to my spinal cord.

Wish number 2 at this point should be self-evident. I mean, I'm named *Franny*. When was the last time you met someone named Franny? Never. Why? Because people named Franny are not fourteen-year-old, not-quite-five-foot semi-pygmies who can't reach their locker dials. Most people named Franny are either 1) tired waitresses at hardscrabble truck-stop diners with nicotine stains on their fingers; or 2) plump, plummy middle-aged British academics who teach Latin and live in tiny thatched cottages with cats named Abelard and Heloise; or 3) elderly, salt-of-the-earth types who had to go to work as secretaries to support their families after their husbands died in World War II.

When I was younger, I assumed my name was Frances and that I could choose another abbreviation. So I thought it would be kind of cool to go by *France*. You know, Bastille Day, champagne, the Riviera, brie . . . But it turns out that my name is not even Frances. It's just Franny. That's it. *Finito*. So is it any surprise that I've ended up being, well, kind of a dork? It's practically a self-fulfilling prophecy when you name an innocent newborn Franny. The only thing worse than the name Franny is—well, I shouldn't even have to say it.

Fran.

Ewwww.

At any rate, suppose I were to tell my genie that I wanted to be named something else. That should be OK, because the name Franny is my burden and no one else I know has to go through life with this name. But every time I mention not liking my name, my dad looks very, very sad, and I know he is thinking about my mom, who is a cultural anthropologist doing fieldwork in Kenya right now. Then he says, "Your mother and I named you after one of the most iconic female heroines of all literature." Then I get all guilty because I have reminded him that my mother is so busy studying the coming-of-age rituals of complete strangers that she is missing the coming-of-age of her own children.

So, yeah, genie, forget wish number 2. I'll deal with Franny. Although I do think that maybe if I had just one pair of dark-wash Miss Sixty jeans it would negate some of the Franny-ness of my life. But when I showed them online to Dad, he said, "One-hundred and ninety-nine dollars?" And then he said my tuition was catapulting him into a "stratosphere of anxiety." As if I *asked* to be incarcerated in that place.

Wish number 3: At this point, you probably assume that I wish my mother would come home and we could live all like a happy family again. Not exactly. That's so after-school special. I mean, of course I'd rather she be here, but I know that this is what she needs to do to finish the book that she's writing. So, fine. I totally get that.

So wish number 3 is simply that the genetic goods were distributed a little more evenly between my sister and me. Because in addition to the better name, my sister, Zooey, also managed to hit the Ford family DNA jackpot.

Here's the deal with my family and our weirdo names. My dad met my mom at this party in college. My mom was artsy and beret-wearing, and my dad was faux-Eurotrash sophisticated and she told him her favorite book was *Franny and Zooey.* He had never read it but pretended he had. Except then she wanted to talk about the book and he couldn't, really, so she knew he was lying. After the party, he got the book and loved it and wanted to talk to my mom about it, except by that point she thought he was a real fake.

At any rate, they still ended up getting together and married and all that mushy stuff, and then they had my sister, Zooey.

Then, nineteen months later, they had me. In case you don't know about *Franny and Zooey*, which is by J. D. Salinger, the same guy who wrote *The Catcher in the Rye*, THE WHOLE POINT OF THE BOOK IS THAT FRANNY HAS A NERVOUS BREAKDOWN! Why would anyone name anything, even a fruit fly, after her? That's bad, *bad* juju.

Whenever my mom tells the story, she sort of giggles and says they'd always wanted to name their first baby Zooey (boy or girl; in the book, Zooey's a boy), which meant that naming me Franny was "obvious."

I happen to disagree. There's a kid in my school named Mickey, but his sister is Sarah, not Minnie. And how many times have you met a Jack without a sister Jill? Or Ben, no Jerry? Adam without Eve? It happens in other families *all the time*.

So Zooey got the better name. A lot of the time it seems like she also got everything else better: a full five feet, six inches of height, perfectly springy ringlets, teeth that never needed braces, and skin that never, ever breaks out. This, in and of itself, has made for a lifetime of totally sucky comparisons.

But that's not all. The Zooeyest thing about Zooey is that she's a dancer. Like a really good ballerina, which means forget the E. C. Stanton School because she goes to a special school at Lincoln Center, just for dancers. They have actually made movies about kids at this school. And it's not that I'm jealous or that I want to be a ballet dancer (which I so don't. You should see Zooey's feet. They are so bruised they look like turkey jerky). It's more that I wish I had that one thing that made me special the way ballet does for Zooey. There is nothing like an entire auditorium full of people applauding your sister's existence to make you feel sort of pointless.

So, yeah, if I could, I'd make wish number 3 for Zooey not to be so perfectly perfect in every way. But to wish for Zooey not to be Zooey would just be *wrong*. I don't think I could even say it aloud. That's got to be worse juju than naming a child Franny. So, salaam, genie. Take your lamp and your wishes to someone else. Someone who might be able to put them to good use.

Poof!

chapter 2

My mom is a wonderful person, but none of her good points have ever been household-related. Like, when she was living at home, she could never manage to fold a fitted sheet, no matter how hard she tried, so she got into the habit of just wadding the sheets into big balls and stuffing them in the linen closet. If you opened the door, you could pretty much guarantee a big avalanche of wadded-up sheets would plonk onto your head. My best friend Rhia's mom isn't very good at that stuff either, but they are so outrageously rich that they have a whole staff of people who, among other things—like making sure Rhia has fresh nori rolls in her red lacquer lunchbox—fold their fitted sheets into these compact, perfect squares that stack as neatly on top of each other as Legos. I used to be jealous of the incredible organization of Rhia's house, but now that my mom's been away, I kind of find myself wishing there were still sheet bundles in our linen closet.

Anyway, the point is that my mom so totally stinks at stuff like laundry that it seems like she couldn't possibly be doing it all that often. But since she's been away, I've had to wonder if we were totally unenlightened Beaver Cleaver types, making her do all the housework and not even realizing it. Because when Mom is around, our apartment, though kind of messy, is still hygienic. But now that she has left, it's morphed into a total sty. There are dust bunnies the size of actual bunnies floating across the floor.

All of which means that on the night of my *very first* high school party, I was burrowing through a large mountain of dirty laundry like some kind of crazed fashion groundhog. I was fairly certain Brianna Bronstein had never found herself in such a situation. Presumably, she had a fairy godmother on call for such emergencies.

"What are you doing?" Rhia asked, watching me from the bed. She was attempting to apply a set of fake eyelashes for some reason.

"I've got to find something for the newspaper party tonight." I sniffed my (well, OK, my *dad's*) vintage Led Zeppelin T-shirt, which I had worn last weekend. It was a bit ripe for a repeat performance. "It's at River's apartment."

Rhia propped herself up on her elbows. "And this is practically your only chance for River to see you out of your uniform," she said earnestly. She had managed to get one eyelash attached, and it blinked crookedly at me in a very sad-clown kind of way.

"Um, yeah," I said. "I want something kind of unusual but not too unusual, you know." To prove my point, I dangled a purple velvet tunic covered in mirrors, which had been a gift from my aunt Sonia. "You don't happen to know how to do laundry, do you?"

"You don't?" she asked.

"You seriously know how to do laundry?" Ecstatically, I filled my arms with as much dirty clothing as I could manage and stumbled to the laundry room, trailing shirts and underwear behind me like Gretel and her bread crumbs.

"OK, this"—Rhia gestured at me—"is a total problem."

"I know." I winced. "I just haven't figured everything out yet."

"Well, laundry is not that hard, Franny," Rhia said, dumping soap in and showing me how to work the dials. "But seriously, how are your dad and Zooey getting clean clothes? Like, someone has to be taking care of this stuff, right?"

I shrugged. Rhia's questions fell squarely on the list of Things I Avoid Talking About, which also included my lack of human growth hormone and the possibility that my mother, whom I had not heard from in five whole days, had contracted Rift Valley fever and was dead in a veldt somewhere with ostriches scavenging her extremely long and Chia Pet–esque hair for their nests.

"Wanna order pizza?" I changed the subject.

"OK."

As I was dialing, the front door opened.

"Hi, sports fan," a voice called out.

Rhia stared at me. "Is that your *dad*?" she whispered.

I checked my watch. It was six fifteen. I absolutely could not remember the last time my dad had gotten home this early. Usually, I have the apartment to myself until eight or so, when Zooey gets in. Dad used to get home around eight also, and we'd all have a late dinner together, but lately he's been meandering in more like ten or ten thirty.

"Hi," I called back, raising my eyebrows at Rhia in surprise.

Dad swung into the kitchen, tossing his leather man-purse and a copy of *Men's Vogue* onto a chair.

"Hello, Rhia," he said formally.

"Hi, Mr. Ford." She giggled. I realized, suddenly, that my dad probably had no idea that Rhia had been coming over every afternoon for the past month. That's one nice silver lining to everyone being so busy: I get the apartment all to myself. We can be as loud as we want or play whatever music we want and there's no one to say anything. It's actually kind of great.

"We were ordering pizza," I said. "Do you want some?"

"Oh, I thought we'd all go out for dinner later." Dad opened the cupboard and pulled down a bottle of Scotch.

"OK," I said slowly, hanging the phone up. Behind my dad's back, I could see Rhia making exaggerated shrugging gestures. "I have this party to go to," I added.

"Tonight?"

"Yeah. It's for the newspaper staff."

Dad set down his glass. "Oh, Franny, not tonight."

"Why not?" Since when did my dad care what I did on Friday night?

"Honey, Zooey has a recital tonight. Didn't you get my messages?"

"No," I said uncertainly. I was *so* not going to give up River-the-Fabulous McGee's party to be held captive in a dusty velvet chair watching a bunch of Scrawnatinas.

"When was the last time you were online?" Dad asked, exasperated. "It's been on my Facebook all week."

Sigh. WHY DO I HAVE THE FATHER WHO REFUSES TO ADMIT SOCIAL NETWORKING SITES ARE NOT PART OF HIS GENERATION? I'm sorry, but I supposedly live in the same apartment with my dad and Zooey; I am not going to use the Internet to talk to them. *Especially* not until my dad gets out of the My Chemical Romance and We Luv Hair Gel groups.

And, really, while we're on the topic, *why* is this my family? Why can't I live in some nice, normal town in Iowa with an insurance-salesman dad and an English-teacher mom and a sister whose big claim to fame is that she raises prize pigs for 4-H? Really?

"Rhia, why don't you come to the recital with us? I made reservations for us at a new tapas place in the Village," Dad broke in placatingly. "It's going to be reviewed in *Time Out* next week."

"Dad, I am not going to the recital," I interrupted. "I told you. I have plans tonight."

"Honey, this is important. It's important to me and it's important to Zooey."

"*My* plans are important, too!" My voice came out kind of squeaky.

"Franny, I'm sure they are and had I known about it, we could have talked about this earlier. But this is a big night for Zooey; she's performing at Lincoln Center, and she deserves to have her family there." Dad spoke in his super-gentle, straight-from-self-help-books, nonviolent-communication voice. It was way more annoying than if he just plain yelled, which is what used to happen, before Mom left. But since then Dad had been turning over so many new leaves that he was practically a rake.

"It's not a special night. I've been to a thousand of these things, Dad."

"I want you there and I know Zooey wants you there as well."

"Oh, come on," I snapped. "Zooey couldn't care less."

"Franny, that's not true."

"Yes, it is!" To my horror, I could feel tears springing to my eyes. "She ignores me at these things." Blinking furiously, I turned away from my dad and Rhia. I hate having people see me upset.

"Franny."

"Anyway, why do we always have to do what's important for Zooey?" The words sounded ugly, but now that I had started I couldn't stop.

"Franny," Dad said again.

"Did you even *remember* I joined newspaper? Look, I'm sorry I'm just a kid and not another professional ballerina so you can name-drop to all your fabulous fashion friends about me."

The instant I said it, I regretted it. Dad set down his glass of Scotch with a clink that suddenly seemed very loud in the quiet kitchen.

"I just want to go do something that's important to me," I muttered, embarrassed.

"It's a party?" Dad asked.

I turned back around. "For the newspaper staff."

"How about you go after the recital? Forget dinner. These things don't last that long and I'm sure the party will still be going on. You can stay out late."

"For real?"

"Yeah."

The relief washed over me. My high school social life was not going to be dead on arrival because my sister happened to be able to jump three feet in the air and land on her big toe. Then I remembered my clothing dilemma.

"Can I borrow your Ducati motorcycle T-shirt?"

Dad narrowed his eyes. "Don't push your luck."

chapter 3

Cha-ching!

Once Dad realized that there was no way we could finish doing the laundry before the recital started, he agreed to lend me his Ducati shirt for the party as long as I put on something more formal for the recital. Since my choices were limited to school uniforms or the heinous purple mirrored tunic, I scavenged Zooey's closet. I figured that since it was her recital, she might as well supply me with clothing.

Zooey's room looked nothing like mine. First of all, it was clean. Second, it was *pink.* Third, there was this ancient poster of Baryshnikov hanging over her bed that was practically pornographic. Anyway, Zooey had tons of clean clothes (don't ask me *how*), all folded over padded hangers at impeccable ninety-degree angles. Since she was eight inches taller than I was and tended to dress like Queen Victoria, I went with the only reasonable option: a very boring stretchy black dress that probably would have fit anything in the range of garden gnome to hippopotamus. I tried to talk Rhia into borrowing something also and coming with us, but she flatly refused. I guess there are limits to every friendship.

"You're certainly invited to come," Dad repeated for maybe the twelfth time as we hailed Rhia a cab.

"Oh," Rhia hedged, "I'll just meet Franny at the party later."

"Are you sure?" Dad said.

I pushed Rhia into the car before Dad could say another word. Then I rolled my eyes at him. "People who have a choice in the matter don't go to Lincoln Center on Friday nights," I commented as we hopped into our own taxi.

"Really?" Dad muttered smugly to me, twenty minutes later, as we stood in the jammed entryway to the Koch Theater. "You think *all* these people are forced to be here? *None* of them had any choice in the matter?"

"I guarantee you a significant percentage would rather be watching the Mets game right now."

Dad snorted, rather inelegantly, as a woman approached us. She was what I'd learned to recognize as a classic ballet type: skinny; black-clad; black hair with one dramatic Cruella DeVil streak pulled back into a tight chignon.

"Oh, Mr. Ford," she oozed. "It's so nice to see you again. You know, Zooey's solo has been attracting so much attention. She's just a delight to watch."

"Thank you." Dad preened.

"She's always been one of our stars, but she's just developed so much in the past year," the woman continued. She leaned in closer. "I shouldn't say this, but you know that Arturo Peretti is here tonight."

"Really!" Dad exclaimed. I shifted back and forth uneasily. This was the worst part of Zooey's recitals. The actual ballet-watching was fine; I mean, it may not have been my first choice of Friday night fun, but it was OK. What killed me was the chitchat. If they were to play ballet chatter on the nightly news, the human species would go extinct in about three seconds flat.

The woman nodded at Dad emphatically. "He's bringing his new production of *Romeo and Juliet* here for Christmas. If I could have gotten away, I would have gone to London to see it, but you know how busy we were with the summer tour. Apparently, Covent Garden was just . . ." She paused and shook her head. "Just blown away with the power of it."

"Yes, we read about it," Dad murmured.

"I should not say this, Mr. Ford, I should not." She leaned in even closer. "But the word on the street is that he wants a very young Juliet for the American debut. I wouldn't be surprised if tonight's recital is something of an audition."

"You think Zooey . . . ?" Dad trailed off.

"I wouldn't be surprised."

There was a pause. "She's still a student," Dad said. "Just sixteen."

The woman smiled an eerie smile. "In ballet, it's never been how old you are, but what can you do at the age you are."

Dad looked like he had more to say, but he stopped himself. "Well, it's only a recital tonight," he said. Then he looked at me with a look I've grown to dread over the years. I winced in anticipation.

"Oh, Madame Selina," he said casually. "Have you met our other daughter?"

Madame's penciled brows rose on her high forehead. "I didn't realize Zooey had a sister," she said.

"Franny," I confirmed, holding out my hand. Madame shook it. I could feel her eyes traversing my body, assessing the way my joints connected and the small slump in my shoulders.

"And," she said, in a voice dripping with befuddlement, "what kind of dance do *you* do, Franny?"

Sometimes I wish I came from one of those families like the Brontës or the Williams sisters. You know, a family where *every sister* got to have a talent.

This was probably not the best comparison, but watching Zooey dance was like watching a character in a horror movie get possessed. It was still technically the same person, but the way she acted was so unbelievably different. The Zooey who danced wasn't the same person who snorted like a rhinoceros or who regularly used up the last of the toilet paper without getting a new roll or who, just yesterday, called me a filthmonger when I left the absolute tiniest ice cream drip on the counter. Zooey dancing was, honestly, sort of magical. I think sometimes my life would be easier if I didn't get what the big deal about Zooey is—but I'd have to be an idiot not to see that she jumps that much higher and lands that much lighter and can stretch her legs that much farther than the other girls. All the dancers at her school are good, of course, but Zooey has this extra something that tricks your eyes into watching her.

She had parts in three dances that night, but the big deal was her solo, which was part of a longer dance with maybe ten other girls, all dressed in peaches and yellows. About halfway through, they lined the edges of the stage, and Zooey ran to the center. She wore a gold tutu. There was a sparkling coronet fastened to her hair, and even her shoes were gold, the shimmering ribbons snaking up her legs. The music stopped for just a moment as she raised one arm into a crescent above her head. Beside me, Dad leaned forward in his seat.

I'd been so angry about, well, *everything* lately that I'd forgotten how much I liked to see Zooey dance. Watching her, I felt quiet, like everything around me was slowing, the way a merry-go-round does just before it stops. A small chill ran along the backs of my arms. I realized I was barely breathing, floating along with Zo as she wafted into the air and landed as lightly as a bubble on the stage.

Zooey used to be my best friend. We shared a room and went to the same school and had this whole play-world we created where we pretended we were mice or orphans in *Annie* or Rockettes. And even when she started taking ballet, it was just something she did and I didn't, the way I liked reading and she didn't. But then she just kept dancing more and more, and somehow I got left behind when she started going to her new ballet school and making new ballet friends and wearing only leotards and tights instead of normal clothes.

Ballet was what had taken us apart, but now, weirdly, the only time I ever felt close to Zooey was when I watched her dance.

chapter 4

"She hit it out of the park," Dad said. We were in the atrium of the theater, waiting for Zooey to come out of the dressing room. The room had exploded with people and conversations bubbled loudly around us.

Because I couldn't exactly explain why watching Zooey dance affected me as much as it did, I just answered, "Yeah." We waited a long time in the crowded atrium before Madame Selina buzzed past us, pointing to Zooey, who was just coming through the stage door. Her arms were full of flowers, and she could barely move through the throngs of people congratulating her. Dad raised one hand in the air and flapped it back and forth so she could see us.

"Sports fan," he called out, but Zooey didn't notice, just kept talking to other people. Sometimes (OK, *often*) I wished my dad could find a way to talk that didn't involve the baseball metaphor. Neither Zooey nor I are actually sports fans, unless you consider Lifetime television watching a sport.

"Should we go over?" I asked. Something about our standing there while crowds of strangers flocked around Zooey on the other side of the room was making me sad.

"She'll get here," he said, continuing to flap his hand energetically. And, after only about ten thousand more air kisses, she did.

"Dad!" she cried.

"You hit it out of the park, kiddo!" he repeated, sweeping her up into a huge hug and crushing the flowers in her arms, just a little. I shifted back and forth.

"There are so many people here," she gushed. "I can't believe it!"

"You were great," I said. "Congratulations."

"Thanks," she answered automatically. Then she looked at me and her face changed. "That better not be Dominique's new dress you're wearing," she said bluntly.

Oops.

Mega-freaking-strike-me-down-with-a-lightning-bolt oops.

"Well," I stalled.

Zooey planted one of her talented feet in front of her and leaned on it menacingly. "Franny Ford, did you or did you not go into my closet and borrow a dress without asking? A dress that had you asked, I would have told you cost my friend Dominique a small fortune and which she only lent me on the absolute promise that I would take the very best care of it, which does not include my filthmonger little sister borrowing it without permission and getting subway scum and food dribbles all over it."

"Well," I said again, "I guess so. But just because it was the only thing that you had that would fit me and I didn't have any clean clothes."

Zooey threw her head backward so that her perfect coffee-colored curls bounced against her shoulder blades. "Daaad!" she howled. I revisited my theory that watching Zooey dance was like watching a satanic possession. Probably she was already possessed and dancing was only a temporary exorcism.

"Sorry!" I backpedaled. "I'm *really* sorry. I was going to change anyway. Honestly. In fact, I'm going to do it now. If Dad hadn't forced me to come, I'd already be at this party right now." *And, frankly, enjoying myself a whole lot more,* I added in my head.

"Party?" Zooey asked.

"Impossible as it may seem, I *do* have a social life on rare occasions," I said with exasperation, grabbing my backpack off the floor and heading to the bathroom, an angry red flush spreading through me. Another cosmic injustice between Zooey and me is that I am the one with the blushing problem. Humans are supposedly seventy-five percent water, but I am probably somewhere in the realm of seventy-five percent tomato juice.

Once safely in the bathroom, I texted Rhia that I'd be at her place to pick her up soon. Then I shed the black dress and changed into Dad's T-shirt and my combat boots. The T-shirt was enormous, hanging well past my knees, so I wrapped Rhia's studded leather belt around my waist and added an extra coat of eyeliner for good measure. Sometimes I can have a bit of an eyeliner addiction.

"Franny Ford, what are you wearing?" Zooey gasped when I reappeared in the atrium.

"I think the kid looks great," Dad said conversationally, as though I weren't standing right there.

"Dad, she has on no pants," Zooey repeated. It amazed me that she had lived through sixteen years of life and still expected my father to act as jolly and concerned as a sitcom dad. I mean, he owns a shop downtown where the mannequins are actually dressed like Elvis in *Viva Las Vegas*.

Dad didn't disappoint. He said, "Sports fan, if a single drop of anything—including water—touches that shirt, you are responsible for finding me replacement pre-1990 motorcycle gear, and I'm warning you that the only acceptable brands are Triumph, Ducati, or Norton."

"And Harley?" I asked, because it was the only motorcycle brand I knew.

Dad shuddered. "American. Really, Franny."

Unlike everyone else I knew, River McGee did not live in a large doorman building on the Upper East or West Side but in a small apartment on the first floor of a brownstone a little past Washington Square Park. There was an actual garden behind the apartment, where everyone was congregated. Even though the party was supposedly for the newspaper staff, it felt like half the school (the older half) was there. River himself was sitting on top of a picnic table that had been painted purple. My hormones began a small riot within my bloodstream. Just as I was pondering the odds of having our eyes lock across the crowded garden, River spotted me and gave me a small, two-fingered salute.

"See, we have a connection," I explained to Rhia, fluttering my fingers back. "How many first-years do you suppose he knows?"

"He just seems kind of full of himself sometimes," she demurred. Well, if anyone had the right to be the teensiest bit conceited, it was River. The boy was a journalist and *trained* to be perceptive; why not start with accurately perceiving himself?

"I'm going to say hi," I said. Rhia shrugged. Slowly, I worked my way through the crowd to the picnic table.

"Hi," I chirped, looking up at River.

"Hey," he drawled. "You made it. Awesome."

"Just barely. I had to go by Lincoln Center first and watch my sister dance." Ew. Why had I brought up Zooey? I mean, *Zooey*. "I'm, uh, not so much the ballet type," I backtracked.

"My sister's in France for study abroad and we're stuck hosting this French student here for an entire year. He can't believe that we don't have any crème fraîche in our place."

"Well, he should never see our kitchen, then, since we store our takeout menus in the vegetable drawer." I paused. "Do you ever think that if there was like, I don't know, a lottery of life and you got to pick your family that you maybe actually wouldn't pick your own?" I stopped. "I mean, I know that's *awful*."

River lowered his eyes briefly, so that his very long lashes were on full display. Then he grinned at me. "You keep thinking stuff like that, Franny Ford, and you're going to get reincarnated as a cockroach one of these days."

Before I could muster a suitably witty (or *any*) reply, Brianna Bronstein materialized between us.

"Baby," she squealed, planting her lips against River's.

OK, she was technically his girlfriend. But still. There was some serious tonguing going on. Like, enough that I was probably in the process of being traumatized and would be having flashbacks of this moment for the next ten years.

"Well, um, thanks for inviting me," I said inarticulately.

River detached his lips briefly and took a deep swallow of air. "Sure, yeah." Then he plunged his lips back onto Brianna's overly slicked ones.

Backing away, I looked around for Rhia, but didn't see her anywhere. I also couldn't find anyone else I recognized. Feeling sort of conspicuously alone, I started toward the food table. I was pouring myself a Coke when a lanky, silky-haired guy appeared next to me.

"Franny, right?"

"Yeah," I answered.

"We're on newspaper together." He paused. "I'm Carter. Carter Cohen-Chang?"

Dimly, in the recesses of my River-obsessed brain, a bell began to toll. "Sure," I said. "Of course."

"I don't know that we've ever really met," Carter said, taking the Coke bottle to pour himself a cup.

"Sure," I repeated, taking a closer look at Carter, who was wearing some form of deconstructed clothing and had a piercing right at the top of his ear, through the cartilage. That's supposedly the most painful place you can ever get pierced. It looked pretty cool, and I normally would have found it a lot cooler, except Dad had recently been talking about getting a piercing in that part of his ear. And, obviously, if my *dad* got pierced, I would be left no choice but to go down to City Hall and become an emancipated minor. Immediately.

"Yo, Carter," a voice called, just then. "Help me move this table. Party needs a dance space." River stood beside us, brushing the long fringe from his eyes. "You help us too, Franny."

Gamely, Carter and I lifted one end of the table as River and another guy grabbed the other. Haltingly, we lugged it through the backyard. I could feel sweat beginning to bead on my forehead.

"Ooooph," I gasped as we set the table down.

"Ooooph?" Carter echoed teasingly, as he shrugged out of his deconstructed jacket. As he did, a set of keys fell to the ground with a clink.

"I'll get them," I said automatically, bending down to root through the dark grass. Somehow, as I combed the ground for the keys and River pondered the exact right location for the table, a hundred pounds of solid hardwood, punch bowls, and drink bottles got lifted again and dropped directly on my hand.

"Oooooph!" I said again, this time almost screaming. It took a special talent to get *literally* pinned to the ground at your very first high school party. "Get the table up!" I squealed, tears springing to my eyes.

"Sorry, Franny!"

"Yeah, dude, we're sorry."

Biting my lip to keep from crying, I examined my hand. The table had come down right across my fingers. Even in the dark, I could see they were purple and starting to swell. A raised whitened ridge, like a caterpillar, striped across them. Gently, I stroked the ridge with my other hand.

"Are you OK?" Carter asked, coming to stand behind me.

I held my purple-fingered hand in the air. "How am I going

to type brilliant articles with this?" I said as breezily as I could manage through the pain.

"And silly me was wondering how you were going to give people the finger," Carter answered.

I giggled. "That too."

"You want to find an ice pack?"

"Sure." As we turned toward the house, I noticed that River had already started dancing with Brianna. His non-puffy hands wrapped around the small of her back as they bounced back and forth to the music. I felt a small sharpness somewhere in the region of my heart.

The facts were clear. In the romantic *Wheel of Fortune*, I had just lost a turn and Brianna had Vanna White clapping overtime.

chapter 5

Rhia's mom was named Mary Ann Zawadski, but she had written many, many novels under the pen name Cynara Jayde Sinclair. The best, in my opinion, was *The Contessa's Pet Rogue*, in which Contessa Elisabetta Sophia da Fiorenza escaped her loveless arranged marriage by running off to the Italian Alps with an olive harvester. Now Mary Ann was concocting something about medieval Scotland. Since it was apparently impossible to write about windswept moors without looking at them, she had whisked Rhia off to Scotland *the day before a geometry test.* Yes, in the middle of the week, in the middle of the term. Talk about a woman with priorities.

Anyway, this left me alone without my normal study buddy. Since Rhia got geometry the way other people got breathing, studying was slow going without her. After working for two hours, I felt like I'd have a better shot *walking* to Scotland than I would passing the test. Frustrated, I flexed my still-swollen fingers and wondered if I could claim I was too injured to write. Then the front door to our apartment flew open with a clatter.

"*Rooooomeo, Roooooooomeo!*" Zooey screamed, leaping into the kitchen, both legs outstretched. She did a quick pirouette. "Wherefore art thou, Romeo?" she asked, pausing to raise one leg above her head and stretching into a rather generous standing split beside me. "Wherefore art thou?"

"Very elegant," I said to her eye-level, leotarded groin. *Saved by the gyrating ballerina* didn't have quite the same ring as *saved by the bell.*

"Don't," Zooey did a pirouette, "be," another pirouette, "a," pirouette, "BUTT!" She stopped and began to curtsey. "Yes, thank you, thank you, thank you very much." She shook her head gracefully, a queen deigning to meet her subjects. "You *are* looking at the new Juliet of Arturo Peretti's ballet."

"Oh, cool," I said. "That's great, Zooey. Congrats."

Zooey stared at me. "Congrats?" she echoed sarcastically.

I shrugged. "Yeah, congrats."

"God, Franny," Zooey answered. "You don't get it, do you?" Her nose curled into a little sneer.

"What?" I asked. Like, really, *what did I do now*? "It's terrific."

Zooey balanced on one toe and began kicking the other foot toward me in perfect rhythm. It was probably a ballet exercise, but it looked kind of aggressive. "This is only like the biggest thing to happen to me in, oh, *ever.*" Kick. Kick. "People would give kidneys for this chance. Would it kill you to show some excitement?"

"I said 'congrats,' like three times," I defended myself.

"In this totally deadpan, don't-bother-me voice."

"Zooey, I'm excited for you. Really. Come on, what do you want?" I looked at her unhappy face. "Do you want dinner? Here's some sushi." I pushed the leftovers of my dinner toward her.

"God! When will you learn that I don't eat anything that once had a *face*?" Zooey stalked out of the kitchen. A few seconds later, I heard a door slam.

Sigh.

Why did I even have to have a family? I mean, why couldn't I be an orphan adopted by some kindly aristocrat, like in a Gothic novel? Then I wouldn't even have to learn about my true family until my eighteenth birthday. And, at that point, I'd have had so many years of wealth and etiquette lessons poured into me that it would only cause the merest, flickering wrinkle of disdain when

I heard that my parents were rank sheepherders living in a mud hut and that my sister had passed from the bloody flux shortly before her fourth birthday.

Zooey didn't emerge until much later that night. "Well, at least *Mom* was excited for me," she announced, delicately stepping into my room, balanced barefoot on her pointes.

I nearly spilled the bottle of nail polish I was smearing inexpertly over my own toes. "You talked to Mom?" I asked, forcing myself to sound casual.

"Yeah, she was *so* thrilled. She said she might come back for opening night."

"Really?"

"Yeah. Her work is going great, too. She says she's going to observe a female circumcision ceremony."

Gross. If being disgusting were an Olympic sport, my mom had just scored a perfect ten for both technical and artistic merit.

Aloud, I said, "That's disgusting." Then, "Do you think she's still around if I wanted to call?"

"Franny, it's like three in the morning there. Don't wake her up."

"You did," I stated the obvious.

"Yeah, but I had an important *reason*. Do you have anything important going on?" Zooey rolled her eyes.

Well, yeah. Let's start with the fact that we were in our fourth edition of the newspaper and I had not yet come up with the set of brilliant ideas that would get River to notice me. Or that I was only four feet, ten inches tall, which according to WebMD could be a sign of no fewer than *three hundred and twelve* grave medical conditions. Or even that I had somehow managed to get a D—yes, a *D*—on an English pop quiz earlier this week because I had been so bored with *The Call of the Wild* that I hadn't exactly read the whole thing. Or, in fact, anything past page ten.

(I *had* tried to suggest to Ms. Hurley, who had kept me after class to ask what was going on, that she revise the reading list to include books teens might actually enjoy—like *The Contessa's Pet Rogue.* Ms. Hurley said that she thought that would be too graphic. As if people getting torn apart by a *dog* didn't count as graphic?)

Anyway, maybe my problems weren't red-alert, major-crisis things that you flew across a planet or woke people up at three A.M. for, but you'd think that they would be something any normal mom would care about. Aloud, I said, as scornfully as I could manage, "Sure, I have, um, stuff, you know."

Zooey didn't even bother to reply. Instead, she looked down at my feet, which miraculously had only a little bit of polish smeared on the cuticles. They actually looked pretty good. "I wish I could get a pedicure sometime," she said. "But it would just be so pointless." She did a quick little leap in the air and picked her way out of the room, still on her nauseating toes.

chapter 6

So Zooey was right. I hadn't realized what a big deal this whole *Romeo and Juliet* thing was until it, well, became a tremendous deal. This wasn't because I was trying to be some evil sister with the sensitivity of a gnat. It was just because Zooey always had some new dance role we were supposed to be excited about. I didn't catch on quickly enough that this *particular* role was different. But then there was a whole photo shoot with *Dance* magazine, for which Zooey had to get all new leotards (a topic apparently worth several hours of discussion). And, once the photos came back, Dad decided that he might as well display some of them in his store windows behind the mannequins, since he liked to change the display once a month anyway. Then, the *Times* decided they wanted to do a feature on Arturo Peretti, who it turned out was the King of the Ballet Universe, so they went to a rehearsal and took a photo of him that also happened to include Zooey, and put it in the paper.

As if all that weren't enough to take an entire bakery's worth of cakes, these big posters of Zooey and the guy who danced Romeo (who was like *thirty* and looked not insignificantly like Brad Pitt in *Troy*) got plastered all over the city with the tagline, "*Romeo and Juliet*: See it again for the first time." So I was confronted with Zooey's perfectly cylindrical thighs about twenty times a day, including twice on the way to school and three times on the way home. Which was definitely more times than I saw Zooey's thighs—or any other part of her—in person, since she was home even less than usual.

If only I were old enough to join the army.

"So, kiddo," Dad announced one night after he called Zen Palate to deliver Zooey's Shredded Heaven soy and gluten platter so she could have it as soon as she walked in the door, "what do you think about having a party for Zooey to celebrate the show when it opens?"

"Sure," I answered.

"I want something special. I was thinking maybe we could do it at the store. If we move the clothes into the storeroom, there'd be plenty of space and we could go all out with the decorating. We could get poster-size blowups of the dancers to hang on the walls."

"Yeah, and you could dangle pointe shoes from the rafters. Like a mobile? It'd look cool."

"Calder-esque, Franny," Dad corrected. "Not *cool*."

"Calder-esque," I said, rolling my eyes. Then I added dramatically, "Mahvelous, dahling."

Dad reached out and messed up my hair. "I like the pointe shoes idea." His eyes flicked over me thoughtfully. "Hey, what's going on with you, Ms. Franny Ford?"

"Nothing." I shrugged. "Promise."

"You're sure? I feel like we haven't had a chance to catch up in a while."

I shrugged. "It's fine."

"You know, sweetheart, we can have a party for you sometime too."

A pity party. My trendster dad *literally* wanted to throw me a pity party.

"For your birthday or something." Dad continued. "Because I want you to know that you're special too."

"Have you been talking to Mom lately?" I asked suspiciously.

"Why?"

"Because Mom was always able to make me feel special without having to *say* it really obviously." Once I said it, I wished I hadn't.

There was a pause, then Dad sighed. "I know, sports fan."

We sat there awkwardly for what seemed like a really long time. Our family is not so much into that whole sharing-feelings thing.

After a long time, the front door opened and Zooey came in. Glad for the distraction, I moved over so she could have some room on the couch.

"I'm so beat," she moaned, flopping next to me. "Maestro gave me a ride home in his car service." Maestro was what Zooey called Arturo Peretti. "I ache all over." She flopped even more dramatically. "Ache. Ache. *Ache*."

Dad got up and filled Zooey's footbath with hot water and these special foaming salts and put it in front of her. "I'll call Zen Palate again," he said. "They should have come by now." He wandered into the kitchen. Zooey pulled off her socks. Her toes were bleeding, and there was a large exposed sore on the side of one of her feet.

"Zooey!" I exclaimed.

"What?" She plunged her feet into the footbath and watched as the foam turned pinkish.

"Your feet are all bloody."

She made a face. "Well, duh. That's what happens when you're a ballerina."

"Well, I know," I said. "But your feet haven't ever looked like *that* before."

"Well, I've never been Juliet in an Arturo Peretti production at the Met either," she answered snottily. Then her face changed. "Don't tell Dad, OK? He'll just freak out."

"OK." I looked down at the pink bubbles. "Are you sure you're OK?"

"Lay off, Franny. Really."

"But . . ." I stopped as Dad came back in. "Dad and I were talking," I said instead. I looked at Dad and he nodded. "About having a party for you."

"To celebrate your first big role," Dad said.

"Well, there's an opening night gala already," Zooey said.

"Another night then," Dad continued. "We want to do something special to mark the occasion." He looked suspiciously misty, like maybe he was actually so overcome with pride that he might tear up.

Zooey shrugged. "That's nice, Daddy, but don't worry about it. Seriously. I'm going to want to get lots of sleep and take care of myself and focus on the production. I don't want to have to worry about a party too."

"Well, you wouldn't have to *worry* about it," he broke in. "We'd be taking care of everything."

"I said no." She looked upset. "Please. Really, just don't. I don't want a fuss." Her face changed. "I think I hear someone at the door. Do you think that's my dinner?"

Because the homework elves had not come and magically implanted facts about *The Grapes of Wrath* in my brain, I had to have another chat with Ms. Hurley.

"Franny, I have to tell you I'm surprised." She brandished my pop quiz, which had another flagrant red D on it.

"Sorry," I ventured feebly. When I realized I wasn't going to be able to identify the speaker of quote with any certainty, I had just left the questions blank. Now I wished I'd at least tried to come up with an answer.

"What confuses me, Franny," she said, sitting on top of her desk, "is that you don't strike me as the kind of person who dislikes books."

"I'm not," I said, taken aback. "I actually read a lot."

"And you're the only first-year to join newspaper, so you must enjoy writing."

"Well," I answered honestly, forgetting that I was in trouble, "I'm not actually writing anything. I mostly just sit there during staff meetings."

"Why?"

I shrugged. "Look, I'm sorry I haven't been doing my best in this class."

"I think you're putting it mildly. I looked at your grades from the last three years, and you've had a straight-A average in English up until this point."

I shrugged again. Nothing like pulling out the snotty teenager act in times of need.

"Is this really about not liking the books we read? I find it hard to believe that you haven't encountered writing you didn't enjoy before."

Shrug. "So I'm not living up to my potential," I said. Even though I was acting all bold, I sort of felt like I might cry. I'm not the kind of kid who gets D's. I'm the kid who gets made fun of by kids who make D's.

Ms. Hurley crossed her legs into lotus style.

"I happened to see this in the *Times*," she said, passing me a clipping of the story about Arturo Peretti that had come out a couple of weeks ago. There was a huge picture of him adjusting Zooey's leg as she stood on one toe. The caption read, "Mr. Peretti took a risk casting his new Juliet, sixteen-year-old ballet student Zooey Ford."

I didn't say anything.

"I put two and two together," Ms. Hurley said.

"Zooey has nothing to do with why I'm not doing well on my pop quizzes."

Ms. Hurley ignored this. "Your parents must have been Salinger fans," she said instead. "Have you ever read *Franny and Zooey*?"

People are always asking me this—like Zooey and I should be into something just because our parents liked it twenty years ago.

"I know what it's about," I told Ms. Hurley. "It's about a girl named Franny having a nervous breakdown."

"It's about families," she said meaningfully, "and wanting people to be different than they are." She paused. "I'll make a deal with you, Franny Ford. You write me a thoughtful paper about *Franny and Zooey* and I will erase these two"—she waved my pop quiz in the air—"D's you've gotten."

I didn't say anything.

"Bonus points if you can convince me you actually liked the book."

"Thanks." I paused. "But I'll just take the D's. I mean, I earned them. I haven't been doing the reading very carefully."

"Don't be a martyr about this. You have until the end of the semester."

"Thanks," I said again, to be polite. But I knew I wouldn't read it.

chapter 7

When I got home, the front door to the apartment was unlocked, which it shouldn't have been.

"Hi," I called out, moving into the empty living room. "Hello." I walked down the hall until I heard sounds coming from Zooey's room. Confused, I stood outside the door for a minute, listening to a cluster of angry voices.

"I will be fine as of March," I heard Zooey announce defiantly.

"Bella, this is not your decision," a gentle Italian voice murmured.

"I want this role. This is my role and I'm good at it," Zooey said.

"Bella, be reasonable. The production is around the corner. We cannot wait."

I felt cold. I stepped closer to the doorway.

"You are talented, my *piccola*. You know that. I will remember you and I will be back for you for some other role. This is not the time."

"No," Zooey cried. I could hear the tears in her voice. "It's not *fair*."

"No. It is not fair," the smooth voice agreed. I wasn't sure what to do. I felt weird eavesdropping, but I felt a good deal weirder just leaving Zooey there to deal with this on her own. I stepped into the doorway and realized, with shock, that the room was filled with people. Like a *lot* of people, all with huge staring eyes and clenched teeth. Zooey was sitting on her bed, tears streaming down her face. She had obviously been crying for a while, because her face was all red and her neck and even her shoulders were wet from tears. My dad was sitting beside her, his arms gingerly around her shoulders, looking like he would rather be just about anywhere else on the planet.

"This is not the end," said a short round man, dressed all in black. His voice was the smooth, caramelly one I had heard through the door. I assumed he was Arturo Peretti. "Good-bye, my girl," he said, with surprising calmness. "You did well."

He walked to Zooey and kissed her cheek. Slowly, one by one, the other people somberly followed him to the doorway. "Pardon," he said elegantly to me, and I stepped aside to let them through.

"What's going on?" I asked.

"Get out of here, Franny," Zooey spat out. "This isn't about you."

"Are you OK? Dad?"

"Maybe you better leave us alone, Franny," he answered. I could hear the distant click of the front door closing.

"But I don't understand what's going on."

"Well, that's because it's none of your business," Zooey snapped. She was shaking as she spoke. Dad moved closer to her and held her closely. "Sports fan, just give us a minute," he said to me.

"It's not fair." I could hear Zooey choke through sobs that were hoarse and desperate. As she leaned closer to Dad, the covers fell away from her lap and I saw a huge and very white cast covering her leg from ankle to mid-thigh. "I said the lift felt wrong. I told them and they kept saying that I should trust the steps and I said it felt wrong and I was *right*," she blubbered into Dad's shoulder. I could see tears on his face as he cradled her. Slowly, I backed out of the room, feeling very scared and confused and very, very alone.

chapter 8

When you call a satellite phone that rings in a homemade tent in the Great Rift Valley at midnight, you run the risk that the person on the other end of the line is going to be a real grouch.

"Dr. Ford," I repeated for the third time. "I want to talk to Dr. Marilee Ford."

Even though the person who answered was roughly fourteen thousand miles away, he exuded a thoroughly jaded, black-rimmed-geeky-glasses sort of vibe. "I assume you are aware of the time difference between America and Kenya?" he drawled.

"Yes," I sighed. "Look, it's her daughter. Can you just please get her? Please?"

"There are five other people sleeping in that tent and I will need to disturb them *all* to get your mother. Just so you know. Not that that's a problem or anything." He paused, then emphasized, "*For you!*"

"Thanks," I said to the empty line. Now that I was in my bedroom, I couldn't hear Zooey crying anymore. It was super-quiet, the sort of eerie silence that made me want to blast raucous punk music.

"Zooey?" Mom's voice came through the phone line, rich and concerned and a little staticky. "Oh, darling."

"It's Franny," I said flatly.

"Franny!" Her voice changed. "I just assumed, I'm sorry," she backtracked.

"So you know about Zooey?" I asked.

"I talked to her when she was at the hospital. How are things going?"

"Awful." My voice cracked. "What happened? No one will tell me anything."

"Well, she broke her leg at practice," Mom explained. "She was being lifted by her partner in a pas de deux and essentially, he dropped her. It was an overhead lift, so she fell about six feet before she crashed on the stage."

I winced at the image. "I think maybe they're not going to let her be Juliet anymore," I said, putting this news together with what I'd overheard.

Mom sighed. "I figured that would happen. Obviously, they can't stop the production."

"She's so upset." I stopped. "Is she going to be OK? She's not, like, *maimed* or anything, right?"

Mom laughed. "No, honey, of course not."

"Oh." I felt better.

"I think we're all upset she'll miss this chance—and she's going to need months of intensive physical therapy," Mom continued reasonably. "It's one of the most unfair things I could ever imagine. Anyway, tell me about you. How's school?"

"Boring."

"I can't believe I'm missing your first semester of high school."

"It's not so interesting," I answered, deciding not to mention that I couldn't believe she was missing my first semester of high school either.

"You know, the girls here remind me of you and Zooey."

"Yeah," I muttered.

"None of them can believe I have kids so young; I'm almost as old as their grandmothers. I love getting to know them and their families."

"Sure," I said. Suddenly, I didn't feel like being on the phone anymore. "I want to go see Rhia. Do you think it's OK for me to leave?"

"Sure, honey, why not?"

"I dunno." I stopped. "I miss you a lot."

"I miss you too."

I literally ran the ten blocks to Rhia's, dodging meandering pedestrians, my loafered feet hitting the sidewalk with great and almost painful thumps.

"Miss Franny, look at you!" Graciela clucked as she held the door open for me, my face coated with a thin veneer of sweat.

"Hi," I panted. "Is Rhia here?" She pointed diagonally, which was the way to the room that Mary Ann called her study and Rhia called the "wannabe bordello" because it really did have an awful lot of silk and feathers.

"Whoa," Rhia said as I burst in. "You OK there?"

She was sitting in a big pink chair, holding a champagne flute filled with ginger ale. Mary Ann had a flute full of the real stuff. She was wearing her silk bathrobe, which is what she wore on bad writing days. On good writing days, she had a red plaid flannel robe that, even though it had been washed many times, still had a big coffee stain on it.

"Kind of," I said, realizing that I still had on my school uniform. This was the funny thing about Rhia and her mom. Even though they were really nice and warm and almost never brushed their hair and wore either a bathrobe or (in Rhia's case) a T-shirt that said Little Miss Trouble on it and a pair of track pants, they *still* managed to make me feel underdressed. While Graciela brought me my own flute of ginger ale, I told them about Zooey. I told them everything, including how I had eavesdropped in the hallway and how Zooey had thrown me out of her room and then convulsed in sobs.

"Wow," Rhia said casually. "Sucks to be her."

If jaws could literally drop, mine fell so far that the mandible practically broke through the crust of the earth and plummeted to China.

"It more than sucks," I explained. "Not dancing Juliet means her life is, like, over."

"Oh, she'll dance Juliet at some point, I'm sure," Rhia said, rolling her eyes a little. "Or some other big role. It's not like she's giving up dancing or anything."

"Still," I argued. "This really is huge. It's the biggest deal on the planet. I mean, have you not seen her on the posters in the subway lately? She's *everywhere*."

Mary Ann smiled at me. "You're a good sister, Franny."

I flushed. I wasn't. I was a totally crap sister. Because the truth was that I really didn't care all that much that Zooey wasn't going to be Juliet. I cared more that everything was so chaotic and, well, even more truthfully? What on earth was wrong with me that I could be even *more* jealous of my sister when she was weeping and injured than when she was strong and intact?

I made Cinderella's family look like Peace Prize candidates.

It's just that I could see how this was all going to unfold: the attention, the nurturing, the sympathy, the constant reassurances that everything would be OK, all followed by a glorious return . . .

I realized Rhia and Mary Ann were waiting for me to say something, so in typical Franny fashion, I just shrugged and muttered, "Not really."

chapter 9

Rhia and Mary Ann insisted that I stay for dinner, which was, of course, extremely civilized and did not involve takeout menus and included not merely a main course but also actual side dishes of whole grains and vegetables. Somewhere, the gods of the food pyramid were basking in serious, triangular contentment.

When I got home, all the lights were out. I switched on a lamp in the living room, just so that I wouldn't fall over anything, and realized Dad had been sitting there on the couch. There was a glass of Scotch in front of him.

"Are you just sitting here in the dark?" I asked. "You scared me."

He reached very slowly for his drink and took a deep swallow. "Where," he said, his voice very quiet and controlled and sort of gritty, "the hell have you been?"

"I went to Rhia's." We'd had such a great time at dinner that I'd stopped feeling awful about the Zooey mess. Now it came rushing back, combined with a tiny bit of fear that I knew was silly—because this was my *dad*, after all—but couldn't help feeling anyway.

"Did I tell you could go out? Jesus, Franny, what is *wrong* with you? Your sister shatters her femur and you boogie out of here without a phone call or good-bye."

OK, the man has been home at this time exactly once in the past two months and that was the night of Zooey's recital. I could have had a successful exotic dancing career at the Funtastic Fantasy Palace and he wouldn't know.

"Mom knew where I was," was all I said in response.

"You called Kenya? In the middle of the night? Great. Very considerate."

"Why are you and Zooey allowed to call her whenever for whatever reason and I'm not?" I shot back.

"I am warning you not to push me," he snapped. I noticed his forehead was sort of sweaty. My dad doesn't drink that much—just one Scotch before dinner—but I had a quick moment of wondering if this might not be his first drink of the night.

I've never seen my dad drunk. I'm sure of it.

"I'm not pushing you. All I'm saying is, you don't get to pick and choose when you feel like being a parent," I answered.

Good job. Way to get all *Gilmore Girls*, Franny.

My dad, unfortunately, did not respond with television parental sensitivity. There was no tearful reconciliatory sharing of feelings, accompanied by the swelling guitar chords of a soon-to-be-widely-recognized female folksinger. He slapped his glass against the coffee table and stood up.

"I suggest you get out of here right now, Franny. I don't even want to look at you right now."

I could feel my heart pounding as I ran to my room and slammed the door. It was only when I was safely inside that I realized that now I was the one who was crying.

Neither Dad nor Zooey was awake when I woke up the next morning. I got dressed as quickly as I could, feeling like I was sneaking around my own house. It was early when I got to school, a full half hour before the first bell, so I went to the library and curled up in a big chair.

It's not like I keep a regular journal or anything, but sometimes when I'm upset, I end up taking out a notebook to write down what's going on. Sometimes making a story out of things helps me understand exactly what's bothering me. So that morning, I turned to the back of my geometry notebook and wrote all about Zooey breaking her leg and what had happened with Dad. I'm not sure I really felt any better when I was done, but at least it was something *I* could do, instead of just letting all this stuff swirl around me.

When I'd said everything I could possibly think of to say, there was still time left before class, so I walked over to the block of computers in the center of the room to check my e-mail. "Dex" had sent me a message. That was Dad, and since I felt about as much like dealing with him as with Ms. Hurley (who was lurking in a corner of the room), I didn't even bother to read what he said.

Instead, I e-mailed Mom.

Hi--

I have been thinking a lot about what you said yesterday about how fascinating Kenya is. I have decided it would be a good idea for me to come be a research assistant with you. Rhia travels with her mom all the time and the school considers it educational, so I am sure you wouldn't have to worry about me missing any classes.

Flights to Kenya are very reasonable right now, so I could be there sometime later this week.

I love you.

Franny

Then, because I couldn't stand it, I opened Dad's message. All it was was a little smiley face.

The man read something like five self-help books a week, and he only spoke emoticon?

chapter 10

Serious journalists are committed to their art. They value it above all else. It occupies their active, churning minds in productive and near-constant ways. They develop a keen sense of social perception. They are rarely distracted. They never drool.

Yours truly managed to demonstrate none of the above during the weekly newspaper staff meeting.

"I just want people to feel like they gain something from reading the *Flyer*," River mused. "Like we opened their eyes to really noteworthy conditions at Stanton." He aimlessly ran a pencil across his cheek. I watched it trail over the quiver of bones and head south to his lips. "Caroline?" he asked, looking at the managing editor for ideas. "Or Jonah?" he said to the features editor. They both shrugged blankly. I stopped staring at River's cheekbones and willed my mind into action.

"I mean, we have Brianna's idea about randomly testing the vegan cafeteria products to make sure they're really vegan and there's no, like, sneaky egg or butter in them." He flicked his clove-colored eyes in her direction. "And that could be totally groundbreaking."

Sometimes I worried that Brianna's seventeen-foot-long legs might have pierced River's skull like a hypodermic needle.

"But we could also do so much more than just that," he sighed.

I nodded sympathetically. He was such a dedicated journalist.

"But don't forget," Carter broke in, "that we also have to get together the annual State of Stanton report sometime this month."

River's head snapped upward. "Aw, shoot." He made a face. "Dude, I can't believe I almost forgot about that."

State of Stanton? Were we seceding from the Union?

"Do we *have* to do it?" River finished

Carter raised his eyebrows. "Well, yeah, I think so. I mean, it gets sent to all the trustees and alumni and parents and stuff."

"It's always the most boring article," River complained.

At the risk of calling attention to my first-yearness, I raised my hand. "Sorry, I'm not sure what we're talking about."

"We're talking about a waste of time," River shot back.

I giggled.

Carter smiled at me. "Every year, the paper has to do an update on school finances."

"It's not as bad as River makes it sound," Caroline broke in. "We cover how the school has spent money over the past year. So last year, we talked about the new gym, and the new basketball team uniforms, and we always talk about new school initiatives. There are ways to make it less awful."

School finance? I agreed with River. And not *just* because he had the best cheekbones in the hemisphere. There were simply many more fascinating topics out there. Like, the life cycle of the caterpillar. Or how asphalt was made.

River rubbed a hand over his chin. It made him look scholarly. "Well, we may as well get it over with," he said, scanning the room.

And then it happened. The clove-colored irises centered directly on my face. I could feel my heart beginning to pound reflexively.

"Franny," River said. My name had never sounded more perfect.

"Mm-hmm?"

"I'm going to put you in charge of the State of the Stanton article this year."

Moi?

"Me?" I squeaked. I hadn't written anything yet for the newspaper. In truth, I had barely even *talked* at the staff meetings. And this was an article that would go to hundreds of people—not just students, but alumni and parents.

Hard-core journalists waited years for this kind of chance. I was getting it handed to me for my very first assignment.

"Sure, why not?" River said. "Take a look at what we've done in the past and see if you have any questions."

I nodded. But my mind was already whirling with ideas. And, River had a good point.

Why not me?

I bounced home, picturing River's reaction when he read my take on the State of Stanton article. Maybe, when he read it, he would realize that Brianna was only a distraction and that it was pointless to keep denying his true feelings for me. Really, he just hadn't gotten a chance to know me yet. But once he did, it would be all sunsets and happily ever afters.

Awash in fantasy, I let myself into the apartment.

"Hi, honey, I'm ho-ome," I called out fifties-housewife style to Zooey. There was no answer. In the week since Zooey had broken her leg, I had barely seen her. That was generally fine with me. It was just too weird and sad.

I changed out of my uniform, tossed some leftover pizza in the microwave, and was on the phone with Rhia telling her all about the article when Zooey crutched into the room.

"I *said*, could you shut up?" she announced stormily. "I've only been trying to get your attention for the past half hour."

What?

"You are, like, *screaming*," she continued. "God, Franny, why do you have to talk to your friends all the time? Can you people not survive without squealing at each other for twenty-four hours?"

On the other end of the line, Rhia was saying something that was probably super-important about the new cafeteria. I tried to pay attention, but Zooey was too loud for me to concentrate.

"I need to call you back," I said, cutting Rhia off midstream. Then, I turned to face Zooey. "What's your problem?"

She rolled her eyes. "I live here too. This isn't just your apartment."

What was that supposed to mean? Aloud, I said, "I was just talking to Rhia on the phone."

"Forget it," she said, sounding disgusted. "Where's Dad?"

"Not home yet."

"Did he order Zen Palate for me?"

"I don't know." I shrugged. "Order it yourself."

"There's no dinner for me?"

"Pizza," I said.

Zooey looked disdainful. "I can't eat that. Especially since I'm not in training anymore. Why don't you just inject the fat cells directly into my thighs?" She rolled her eyes. "Not that you would care. I mean, it doesn't matter how much you blimp up."

My slice didn't taste very good anymore. I pushed the plate away.

"Why is Dad *never* home?" she asked.

It was probably a pretty good question, but there were about a thousand things I would rather have been doing at that exact moment than talking to Zooey. Annoyed, I walked out of the kitchen with as precious little stomping as I could muster.

Zooey didn't need to worry about not being able to dance. If there were a universe-wide talent show *tomorrow*, she would still take home top honors for her natural ability to wreck a night in three seconds flat.

chapter 11

Once, when I was a lot younger, there was this time I talked Zooey into playing news reporter. We smeared on all this blue eyeliner and did our hair in massive puffballs and trotted through the lobby of our apartment building with the video camera Mom used for her fieldwork, interviewing whoever happened to walk by.

"Mrs. McGreevey," I'd said to our lavender-haired neighbor with a walker. "Do you feel the homeowners' organization has been receptive to your special needs?"

Or, to the doorman, "Tell us about a day in the life of a Brooklyn resident."

Zooey, behind the camera, would give me thumbs-ups or, occasionally, a little boogie of celebration that was most certainly not a part of the Royal Academy of Dance curriculum.

We had a blast right up until the time Mom decided she needed to review an interview, realized neither her children nor her video camera were around, and actually dialed 911. When the policeman got to the building, Zooey and I pounced on him for an interview. The aftermath was bloody and unpleasant and involved the police officer yelling at my mother that maybe she should actually check her apartment building before declaring a state of emergency.

Anyway—out of coincidence or emotional scarring—I couldn't remember interviewing anyone from that day until the exact moment that I stood in the hallway before homeroom the day after fall break, notebook in hand, the staff camera dangling heavily from a cord around my neck.

"Hi, I'm with the *Flyer*; I'd like to ask you a question," I said ineffectively to the throngs on either side of me. "Hi, I'm Franny; can I ask you a question for the school paper?"

After about ten minutes of people swarming around me, I felt like I was starring in my personal version of human ping-pong.

"Man, you are barking up the wrong tree," a voice said beside me. I turned. It was Carter Cohen-Chang, who had evidently spent his weekend dyeing the front portion of his silky black hair a navy color.

"What?" I answered inarticulately.

"This," he gestured to the packed hallway, "isn't how you get people to talk to you."

"I'm sort of figuring that out." I smiled at him. "It's for that State of Stanton piece." I shrugged. "I thought I'd try to make it a little different this year."

Carter's eyebrows raised. "That article's got an established formula. Aren't you kind of reinventing the wheel?"

"Maybe, but I thought I'd get some candid comments about how people think the school *should* be spending money. So River said just to go into the halls and see what people had to say."

Carter snorted. "Hello? When was the last time that boy was in the field? Kid hasn't written anything other than his editorial letter in a year and a half."

Well. Who ingested too much kryptonite and made him Clark Kent? "He's a great editor," I defended automatically.

"Didn't say he wasn't." Carter shifted his messenger bag a little higher on his shoulder. "Just that this wasn't actually the best way to a great feature."

"So what would a better way be?" I asked, looking at the swarms of people flocking around us.

"Follow me," Carter said. Together, we walked through the

crowded halls, snaking behind the cafeteria, toward the back courtyard, where the smokers hung out.

"Um, Carter, we can't go out there," I said.

"Why not?"

Because it's filled with scary people! That seemed like the sort of dorky thought that should never be said aloud. In a failed attempt to be minimally cooler than I actually was, I came out with something even worse. "Because it's against school rules," I said.

Carter stopped. "You want this story? You want to learn how to talk to people and make them listen and get them to say things that are interesting and not only worth reading, but actually say stuff about our school?"

Yes. For the past week, I'd fallen asleep thinking about the article and woken up thinking about the article. I'd restarted the intro at least three times.

"Yes," I said aloud.

"Then shut up and come on."

Stung, I followed Carter through the back door of the school, into the courtyard. He walked right up to the knot of smokers, who parted to let him in. With his navy forelock and untucked uniform shirt, he fit right in.

"Hey, man," one of them said.

"Hey," Carter answered. "We need you to help us out again."

"Dude, again?" the guy asked, taking a deep drag on his Marlboro.

"Yeah, again. This is Franny. She's one of our new staffers; she's got a few questions for y'all."

"Hi," I said lamely. "I'm doing a feature on how the school decides where money should go, and I wondered if you had any ideas."

The ringleader snickered. "Yeah. I want a six-foot-tall monument to Bob Marley put up in the hallway."

I looked at him dubiously.

"A skate ramp behind the school. A supply of both acoustic and electric guitars in the music room, not just orchestra instruments. A ticket fund so we can go hear live music in the city."

"A better darkroom," a pink-haired girl beside him added.

I reached for my pad and started scribbling.

"Huh," I said to Carter as we headed inside a few minutes later. "They actually had some great ideas."

"I'm not saying 'I told you so.' "

"But . . ." I paused. "Um, *clearly* you are."

He tossed the navy flop from his eyes. "OK, just a little."

"Well, thank you," I said sincerely. "That was great. I think I have enough time to start transcribing this before class."

"But we're not done," he answered.

"No?"

Carter sighed. "Franny, that was only one group of kids. We need a whole range of people in the school. We should probably only use *one* of all those suggestions in the article. Don't you want this to be about everyone in Stanton?"

"Of course."

"Well, come on."

Over the next half hour, Carter and I chatted up pasty-faced computerites in the tech lab, the European espresso-sippers on the front staircase, beefy lacrosse players lifting weights in the gym.

"I can't believe how much easier it was to talk to people with you there," I said to Carter, as we deposited the camera back in the newspaper office.

"Got nothing to do with me and everything to do with catching people once they're where they want to be, rather than delaying them from getting there. Does that makes sense?"

"Yeah." I thought about it for a moment. "Hey, Carter?"

"Yeah?" he echoed.

"This was kind of awesome."

chapter 12

It was a dark and stormy night. For real. Any other time, I might have been spooked by the flickering lights and crashing thunder, but I was too absorbed in my State of Stanton article to notice the weather until my cell phone rang.

"I don't like this thunder," Zooey said.

"Why are you calling me?" I asked. "Aren't you in your room?"

"I didn't feel like getting up," she explained. "My leg hurts. So I called."

"Oh," I answered. "Well, I'm kind of working right now."

"Come work in my room," she said. I looked at all my notes and digital recorder spread out across the floor. They weren't exactly transportable.

"Zooey, it's just rain."

"I'm sure that's what Noah said too!"

I pulled the curtain aside and stared out at the street, where the rain was gusting down in huge sheets. As far as I could tell, the animals had not yet lined up by twosies.

"Zooey, I really need to work on this article for the paper," I said. "I'll come by in a bit."

"You're always working," she said, hanging up on me.

"Think of your favorite things!" I yelled, loud enough for her to hear through the wall. Then I hunched back over the computer.

Zooey was right: I had been working a lot. Somehow, the State of Stanton article had morphed from a chance assignment into a thing that had taken over my life. Barely a night had gone by that I hadn't let myself get sucked into notes and interviews and dense financial statements. I still wasn't fully sure how to get my argument across. After rereading my opening paragraph aimlessly, I reached for my phone.

"Carter?" I asked. "I hope I'm not bothering you."

"Franny, is this about the article?" he said automatically. "At some point, you gotta turn it in."

"I will," I said. "I'm just not sure it's there yet."

"That's what you said last week."

"Well, last week it *really* wasn't there," I defended. Now that I thought about it, I guessed I *had* been calling Carter a lot. He was great about answering questions.

"So what's your question?"

"Right now, I'm thinking of making it about Stanton being different. Do you think that's too . . ." I trailed off. "Too something?"

"Tell me more."

"It's just that Stanton's a school that cares about being different. Like, a lot of kids truly, madly, deeply love the things the school budget supports—the juice bar in the cafeteria or the fact that we have an Anti-Genocidal League for Global Humanity."

Carter made an mm-hmming sort of noise that I took as a sign to continue.

"So, I think different is good. But I only think it's good if you get to know normal."

"Meaning?" Carter asked.

"Part of being in high school is getting to be in that traditional teen world, the way it is in movies, with cheerleaders and pep rallies and marching bands. Stanton is so obsessed with being cool and different that all the school funds get spent so we don't ever get any of the regular parts of high school. So maybe we should start thinking about doing more normal high school stuff. Life gets sort of out of hand when everything and everyone in it has to be special."

The minutes oozed by as he thought.

"Isn't it kind of a big twist to put on the topic of school finances?" he said at last. "This article has a formula and you're really doing something new here."

"River said the old way was boring," I answered.

"What do you think?"

I paused. "Well, I read the reports from the last three years, and yeah, they were kind of dry. But . . ." I trailed off, thinking about the article. "I only want to do this if I can be sure I get it exactly right."

"And that's why you're slaving at it," Carter said. "Because with writing, you can take all the time you want to be sure you're saying what you want to say."

I thought about all the times words had flown out of my mouth and I'd wished I could unsay them. "Exactly," I said as a particularly loud clap of thunder crashed through the air. The lights flickered ominously.

"So tell me more about how you're going to use the interviews," Carter said. "Because they could either really help your argument or end up hurting it."

"Sure," I agreed. Just then, the power finally gave out, throwing the room into darkness. It didn't matter. I was already burning the midnight oil anyway.

chapter 13

If there really was a sucker born every minute, they were evidently all getting born *inside my brain*. There was no other explanation for why I would agree to help Zooey crutch her way downtown to see a dance performance. We hadn't even made it to the elevator before the regrets started kicking in.

"Franny," she ordered bossily. "You need to push the elevator button. You know it's hard for me to do that with my crutches."

"Are you sure we should be going out?" I asked skeptically. "I mean, if you can't make it to the elevator, I don't see how you're going to make it all the way to the theater." I'd finally managed to get my article to River that afternoon. This wasn't exactly my first pick for how to celebrate.

"Franny!" she snapped, holding the elevator door open with one elbow and hopping inside.

"Zooey!" I echoed in exactly the same tone of voice as I followed her into the elevator. "Thank you, Franny," I added, in a syrupy tone of voice, "for giving up your night to go downtown to see dance. I know how much you would rather be out with your friends right now and I also know you have lots of homework and other things to do. I just wanted to let you know how deeply and truly I appreciate it."

Zooey gave me a nasty look. Since I was sort of enjoying myself by this time, I added, "And while we're on the topic, I'm having a custom-craft halo made for you, because you deserve it."

As soon as the doors opened, Zooey booked it, limping through the lobby with lightning speed. This seemed like a good thing.

Because even though I had agreed to go to this performance with her, I'd be lying if I said I was convinced it was all going to go OK. As far as I knew, Zooey hadn't been outside in the weeks since she had broken her leg. Her physical therapist came to our apartment, and the ballet school had just decided to let her do independent study rather than go to classes. From what I had seen, she seemed to be deeply engaged in independently studying the ceiling of her room, with an occasional foray into Lifetime television.

Anyway, the last thing I wanted was for this night to end with Zooey flat on the pavement and writhing in pain because she couldn't really crutch around as well as she thought she could. Thoughtfully, I hailed us a taxi without any more comments. Once we were safely inside, I added, "I'm really OK with going to the ballet with you tonight."

Zooey sniffed. "You should be. Do you have any idea how hard it was to get these tickets?"

Sometimes I think that if Zooey were to win the lottery, she would complain about how she hadn't wanted the money delivered in hundreds. She'd probably send it back so they could change it into twenties. And then, once she realized Andrew Jackson had huge, unsightly pores, she'd send it back to be changed into fives.

It turned out that the performance Zooey wanted to see wasn't even ballet, or at least not the sort of ballet I'd seen her do over the years. The dancers did wear pointe shoes in some scenes, but they also did these incredible circus-y contortions with their bodies and the music was pretty varied: some classical, some rock, and some jangling atonal stuff that I would be perfectly content never to hear again. I didn't dislike it. But I also didn't exactly like it.

When intermission rolled around, I assumed we'd stay in our seats. Zooey thought differently.

"Let's go to the lobby," she suggested, lurching upright by grabbing tightly to the back of the seat in front of her.

"I'm OK staying here," I said, tying my hair back with a ponytail holder I'd found around my wrist. This was code for *You have a cast the size of Bolivia on your leg and it causes you to move more slowly than a snow pea.*

"There may be people I know here," Zooey said. "I want to see them."

I envisioned three weeks without Rhia and flinched. It had never occurred to me that Zooey might miss her friends.

"OK," I agreed, but I was talking to thin air, because Zooey had already started hopping her way slowly down our row.

Trilobites have turned into fossils in less time than it took for us to make our way into the lobby. About halfway there, Zooey stopped for a break, reaching a hand to the wall to stabilize herself. A faint sheen of sweat glistened along her brow bone, and her teeth were clenched. I didn't say anything and neither did she, and a few minutes later, she was swinging along again.

We hadn't been in the lobby for more than a minute or two when two girls approached us. They were both dancerly, wearing exactly the sort of simple, flowing knit dress that Zooey had on, with their hair pulled up into buns, just in case there was any danger they would get mistaken for yogis or (gasp) modern dancers.

"Zooey? I thought it was you," one of them said. But she said it in a way that wasn't exactly shiny-happy.

Zooey smiled in a forced sort of way. "Hi," she squealed. Then, "Franny, you know Dominique, right?" I nodded. "And this is Fiona."

"We didn't expect you to be here," Fiona said to Zooey.

"I got the tickets from school, same as you."

"Sure, of course," Fiona backpedaled. "It's nice to see you."

"I should be dancing again next spring when Gunther choreographs for the company," Zooey justified.

Ahh, that made sense. Of course, there had to be a reason why all these snooty Lincoln Center types had come to see this particular performance.

"I don't think there are going to be parts for students in next spring's show," Dominique cut in.

There was a pause.

"How's everything going at school?" Zooey changed the topic.

Fiona and Dominique exchanged an extremely unsubtle look.

"What?" Zooey said.

"Nothing. School's great!" Fiona covered quickly.

"She'll find out anyway," Dominique said to Fiona. Then, to Zooey, "I haven't been to school much lately because I've been doing all my schoolwork and classes elsewhere," she explained.

"Oh," Zooey said.

"Since I've taken over for you as Juliet," Dominique finished.

"Oh," Zooey repeated.

"They decided not to use the understudy because Maestro wanted someone young and new for the role, someone who had never had a lead professionally before," Fiona broke in.

"Of course." Zooey's voice sounded funny, all flat and metallic, the vocal equivalent of a can of Diet Coke left open and in the rain for a week. "Congratulations."

"Well, when opportunity knocks," Dominique drawled. She fluffed her hair. "Who'd pass up a chance like this? I mean, *you* weren't going to rise from the dead."

Eep. She made Brianna Bronstein seem like Hello Kitty. Zooey looked like she'd been slapped.

"Yeah," I said aloud, surprising myself with the words. "When you look at it that way, it's kind of awesome that Zooey fell.

Imagine if you were still stuck with her getting all the best roles."

Dominique's eyes lingered speculatively on my face, as if deciding whether or not I was worth squashing. "See you around," was all she said, very coolly.

"Wow, she's evil," I said to Zooey after they'd left.

"She's my best friend at school," Zooey answered matter-of-factly.

"Are you *serious*?"

"Dominique taking that role was nothing personal. I mean, I'd do the same if I were her. I wouldn't think about her." Her face scrunched even more. "I guess we can leave," she added. "I've seen everything I needed to."

chapter 14

I slept just awful that night. Maybe there was a pea tucked under my mattress, or maybe I was thinking about Zooey. Anyway, I slugged through the next day as best as I could. By the time I got to newspaper production after school, I thought I might keel over, timber-style. And while I don't know about trees in forests, I assure you that if a Franny fell in the middle of school, she would definitely make a sound.

Production always made normally cucumber-cool River tense. I could tell by the way he pushed his Greek fisherman's cap a little higher on his head and closed his eyes for a moment before beginning to give instructions. "Carter, you proof these sports pages; Caroline, I need you to start the layout for the front page. Franny, can you get the big board going?"

"Sure," I said, reaching for the list of articles we were putting into production that week. Carefully, I lined up the names of the articles on the white board and marked an X to indicate how far each was along. So far, the sports articles were already edited, but nothing else seemed to have much progress. I scanned the list briefly, trying to make sense out of it.

"Hey, River?" I asked, going quietly over to him.

"Yes?" He glanced up briefly from the article he was copy-editing. A small vertical furrow marred his otherwise perfect brow.

"I was just setting up the board," I started. "And I couldn't help but notice that my State of Stanton article wasn't on the production list."

River rubbed a hand briefly across his eyes, like a cat stretching. "Oh. Right." He paused. "Sorry, I meant to talk to you about that before now."

A very cold and wormy feeling began working its way through me. It was sort of like a blush, slow-spreading and all-overish, but much chillier and sicker.

"We can't publish that article."

What?

"Sorry, Franny," he continued, as casually as if he were telling me he'd finished the last of the gummy bears. "I mean, thanks for trying."

"I don't get it," I said, thinking of all the nights I'd spent curled with my laptop and thesaurus, all the help I'd begged from Carter.

"Why?" I added. "Was there something wrong with it?"

"Do you have a copy of the article?" River asked.

I nodded.

River glanced around the humming production room. "I think they can deal without us for bit. Why don't we go get a coffee and talk?"

As we walked silently over to Starbucks, I wanted to say something. But I didn't, and neither did he, until we were settled at a table with our Venti black French roast (for him) and hot cocoa (dopily enough, for me; I think coffee tastes like boiled dirt).

"There was a part of me that totally dug your article, Franny," he started. "For real. It's smart and funny and has this great, opinionated voice and . . ." He paused. "And it's very persuasive."

I felt my lips crinkle as I waited for the flip side.

"But it's not, like, journalism. It's not objective; it deals only with what you think and feel, and you don't present the facts at all—and frankly, I was left trying to figure out the truth of the scenario. If you're a *reporter*, your job is to *report*."

I realize this is astronomically impossible, but I swear the earth actually stopped rotating on its axis for about five whole seconds.

For the record, I am not a crier. That's Zooey. She's the heart-on-the-sleeve one, the sort who's not afraid to bawl or scream or be nasty or sappy or whatever. Her dancing is so filled with whatever she feels that it makes *other* people—people who don't even know her—tear up. That's not me. When I get upset, I kind of freeze and have trouble with the most basic things, like breathing. Talking at times like these isn't merely difficult; it's pretty much impossible.

So when River said that about my article, I just sat there, very still, and let him go on far past the point where I stopped listening. It was like I had turned into a sno-cone. A drippy, inanimate, zero-nutritional-value, falling-apart-the-instant-it's-touched sno-cone.

"Franny?" River asked after talking for what seemed a very long time. "Are you listening?"

I forced a bright smile on my face. "No, I'm fine. I'm listening. Maybe I can work on the article some more? I mean, I just don't want to scrap it entirely."

"Yeah, try to revise it. You get what I'm talking about, right? It's just the *Flyer* saves the soapbox for the editor's letters, not for ordinary news articles." He made a wry motion with his eyes, causing his excessively long eyelashes to flutter. Yes, actually flutter.

"Sure, OK." It was an effort to shove the words out of my lips and into the air, where they lurked, inadequately, between us.

River looked at me for a minute. "You're a cool kid, you know," he said.

Earth to sno-cone! Prepare for melting!

"I wish everyone was as smart as you." He paused and—I kid you not—a small, pale flush spread across his cheeks.

Unbelievable. River McGee was a blusher. We were so similar, and so sensitive, and he said I was a cool kid. I focused my eyes on the small, pinkish indentation in the center of his upper lip. It was what Rhia's mom would describe in a book as "a crevasse of love waiting to be filled."

"I guess we should head back," he muttered.

"Sure," I said dumbly.

It was stupid, but I felt deprived, like maybe I was in a reverse *Wizard of Oz* and instead of finally getting the brain and heart and courage I so desperately needed, I had actually just given them up.

chapter 15

"Franny, are you *sure* everything is OK?" Rhia stared at me across the lunch table.

"I don't know why you keep asking me that. I'm fine; I'm just tired."

Tired didn't really cover it.

"You've barely said a word in the past three days, including when the newspaper came out without your article in it. Your hair is, I'm sorry to say, a big old gross mess, and you said I shouldn't come over after school yesterday because you felt like being alone," Rhia said bluntly.

Oh. Well.

"Franny!" Rhia waved a chopstick under my nose. "Did you hear me? What is going on with you?"

"Nothing." I stood up. "Promise. Look, I think I'm going to the library for a bit. I'll see you later, OK?"

"Well, do you want to come over to my place this afternoon?" Rhia called after me.

I didn't, really. But I didn't know *why* I didn't want to hang out with my best friend, and I also didn't know where else to go or what else to say. So I simply answered, "Yeah, sure."

The library was pretty quiet when I got there. I logged onto Facebook and thought about sending something to my dad (who, it turned out, had recently joined the Let's Outlaw UGGs group) but really couldn't think of anything to say. I sighed and checked my watch. Fifteen minutes before class. Maybe I should have just stayed in the cafeteria.

All of a sudden, I just didn't feel like being in school. It was like I *couldn't* be there anymore, like something awful would happen if I stayed. Without even realizing it, I let my feet take me to the infirmary.

"I'm sick," I announced to the nurse. "I have to go home."

"What's wrong?" she asked.

"I threw up," I lied. "Just now, in the bathroom." It was like I wasn't even conscious of the lie, like the words just came out by themselves and hovered in the air between us.

Automatically, she reached a cool hand to my forehead. "You don't seem to have a fever."

"I threw up," I repeated.

"It could just be something you ate," she said. "You do look a bit clammy. I'll write you a pass."

And then, just like that, I was out of there. It had been so easy. I stared out at the taxis and fruit vendors and meandering throngs of people in bewilderment, not sure of what had just happened. The last thing I wanted was to go home and encounter Zooey, but I didn't really have any other place to go. For lack of a better option, I started walking west and went into the park. That's where jaded New York kids always ended up in books and movies when they cut school in order to mope about the state of their lives.

But, as it turned out, moping wasn't very fun when it was the end of October and the middle of the week and you were cold because you were wearing stupid kneesocks with your school uniform rather than tights. After a much smaller amount of wallowing than the situation deserved, I gave up and scurried over to the zoo. I hadn't been there since I was a lot younger, and it hadn't exactly improved over time. There's not much space, so they can't have many big animals. I just stared at the chimpanzees for a bit and by then it was after two, so I left and started walking downtown.

Very *aimlessly* walking downtown. Think less direction than a whirling dervish. It wasn't until I was past Times Square, a whole mile and some from the park, that I decided to go to Dad's store. It took me almost another half hour to walk there. It was empty inside, almost as empty as the zoo had been. The store had always been cluttery—lots of vintage sunglasses and bowling bags and overpriced distressed T-shirts—but there was definitely a lot less clutter today, and the clothing and displays looked shiny and futuristic.

"Hellooooo," trilled a black-clad woman. She had on these boots, ridiculous ones, which came up all the way over her skinny knees and clamped, via suction only, no zippers, around her mid-thigh. They were not made for walking. "Is there something I can help you with?" she asked in a not very nice way.

When I was a lot younger and Mom was still in school and Zooey was at dance classes, I used to spend a lot of time with Dad at the store. At the time, it was in a much less fancy building. He always managed to have spare mannequins around, and I would dress them up in crazy outfits and give them ridiculous wigs and props, and Dad would put them up in the store, arranging them with the same gravity with which he arranged the front window displays. Once, I did a whole tea party of mannequins with hot pink Mohawks, all holding little rose-patterned china cups in the air. He definitely didn't have *employees* back then.

"My dad is Dexter Ford," I said. I wished I could have sounded as slick as she did, but it came out pretty tentative and stuttery.

"Of course," the woman said smoothly. "Dex," she called. When there was no answer, she slipped past me, murmuring, "I'll just go get him."

While I waited, I looked around. I didn't see the Elvis mannequins anywhere. Dad had had Elvis forever, but now all the mannequins were bald and silver and holding laptops and listening to iPods.

"Sports fan?" Dad said questioningly, walking toward me. He had on a leather shirt. *Leather.* "Everything OK?" Behind him, I could see the woman hovering curiously.

"Where's Elvis?" I asked, gesturing to the new mannequins.

"Oh, I decided it was time for a change. You like it?"

"No. Not really. I liked Elvis."

Dad raised his eyebrows. "Well," he said. "Did you come by just to play fashion critic? Or was there another reason?"

Apparently I couldn't even get *truancy* right, because I had to be the only person dork enough to cut school to go hang out with her dad. I shrugged.

"Anyway," Dad said agreeably. I noticed the shiny-boot woman had taken a few steps forward, so now she was practically right beside us. He looked over at her and smiled, a genuinely warm crinkly smile. When I saw it, I realized I hadn't seen him smile much lately.

"Oh, Fran Sancisco," he said. "Have you met Celia?"

CELIA. HE SMILED A CRINKLY SMILE AT CELIA.

All of a sudden it hit me. I had thought my dad was just working a lot. But all those nights that he'd been at the store or scouring flea markets, he was doing those things with Celia. And her shiny, thigh-high suction boots and her black nails and her caved-in, model-hollow cheeks.

What if he was having an *affair*? And what if that was why Mom had gone to Kenya?

Universe, meet collapsing.

He wouldn't. He just absolutely wouldn't. And not with someone like Celia, who was so tall and fashion-y and . . . standing three inches away from him, gazing adoringly at him with her much mascara-ed eyes. Maybe she was the reason the store looked so different now.

I tried to think of the last time he had talked to Mom and couldn't.

"I didn't know Celia worked here," I said.

Celia pursed her burgundy lips. "It's been almost a year," she said.

"Really?" Dad chimed in. "It feels like you just got here."

I just bet it did. Time was probably flying.

I was going to explode if we didn't change the topic. "I'm hungry," I broke in. "And you forgot to refill the takeout cash drawer so I can't even order." I didn't mean to, but I could feel my face tensing up into a tiny sneer.

Despite—or maybe because of—the leather shirt and flossy silvery store, Dad looked very old of all a sudden. "Aw, Fran, I'm sorry." He reached for his wallet. "I am so sorry." He sighed. Celia moved one micrometer closer to him. They were now practically touching.

"Where'd you get the shirt?" I asked as he rifled through his wallet.

"It's from Bartolomeo; you like it?"

"No." I wasn't sure why I was being mean.

"Really?" Dad sounded surprised. I didn't say anything. "Look, here's some cash for the drawer, and here's a credit card to put in there also, just for emergencies like this, OK?" he added, handing it over to me.

"OK." I looked at him for a second, trying to think of what to say.

Why was it that I turned into a sno-cone during all the most essential moments of my life?

chapter 16

After I left, I felt the worst I had all day, maybe even all year. Rhia had called to find out why I had vanished, but I didn't feel like talking. I turned my cell phone off so I wouldn't hear it if anyone tried to call me again. Then I hopped on the subway, only instead of heading uptown toward home, I went down and got out in the Village.

There are definitely kids at Stanton who are down at St. Mark's Place getting pierced every weekend. But I had a low threshold for pain and an even higher threshold for bad movies and Twizzlers. That meant that wandering around that area was pretty unusual for me. I liked it, though. The streets were packed with thrift stores and people with messenger bags bopping to iPods. Something about the energy made me perk up a little. When I saw a henna parlor, I hesitantly made my way past some dusty candelabra and large vases and a very massive pipe to the back of the store.

"'Allo, beauty," a woman greeted me warmly. She was very large, with a thick red braid and wide smile. Her nose was pierced with a tiny emerald. "You want a tattoo?"

"Please," I said. "Henna wears off, right?"

"Shouldn't last more than a month."

"Great." I took the binder she handed me and began flipping through the designs. I stopped at a picture of a girl with brown wavy hair, like mine, piled on top of her head. Down the back and sides of her neck was an intricate lacy pattern. She looked like the sort of person who had just been running through a meadow with her guitar, someone who maybe had never even been to New York.

"I love that," I said slowly, running my finger across the picture.

"Good choice," the woman agreed. She reached out and touched the side of my neck. "You have a good long neck for it."

There are only two kinds of creatures ever described as having long necks. One is a giraffe and the other is Audrey Hepburn. I hoped I was in the Audrey category.

The woman began pulling over a series of small pots and brushes. She handed me a brush and set of hair combs. I have the sort of hair that you can jab a pencil in and it will stay up forever, so it only took me a second to get it on top of my head. The slow, cold tickle of the alcohol pad ran over my skin. I leaned back and started to relax.

If there is one thing a lacy henna tattoo does not go with, it is a school uniform. *Especially* not the sludge-gray and white kind that looks like it would be more appropriate attire for a Soviet factory than downtown Manhattan. And even though I had to wear this big zombielike bandage on my neck to seal in the henna, I could already feel meadowness seeping through me.

As I walked toward the subway, the stores around me got increasingly posh and the streets less chaotic. I was so busy thinking about how surprised River would be when he saw my fabulously lacy neck that I almost didn't notice the tiny boutique when I walked past it.

Bartolomeo. Aka home of the leather shirt.

I paused for a minute, then went in. Lots of shiny minimalist aluminum and throbbing techno music.

MY DAD SHOPPED HERE?

Duh. Of course he did. In fact, I realized, this was what his new store display was trying to copy. Slowly, I reached out for a black frothy tank top and felt the delicate fabric. Since I still didn't feel like heading home, I pulled the tank top off the rack to try on. I added a few other things and headed back to the dressing room. They were all too big, of course, except one dress. It was black, with cherries on it, and exactly the sort of thing someone with a lacy henna neck would wear. It fit *perfectly.* In it, I somehow looked all tall and delicate and willowy. Speculatively, I checked the price tag.

Peasants had rioted for less.

It was more than a plane ticket to Kenya or, like, *five* orchestra seats to *Romeo and Juliet.* I fingered Dad's credit card. Really, it was the least he could do.

The salesgirl looked at me suspiciously when I brought the dress up to the register. This was a clear case of ageism. I mean, I knew plenty of kids at Stanton who had their own credit cards that their parents paid for. Still, it looked like I might have to work some smoothness over this woman.

"This is my dad's favorite store," I lied casually. "We have a dance coming up and he wanted me to get something special. So he gave me his card and said to come here 'cause he likes the clothes here so much."

The salesgirl smiled and relaxed. "Where are you in school?" she asked, folding the dress within masses of creamy paper.

"E. C. Stanton," I answered, taking the receipt and pen she handed to me. I wasn't sure if I was supposed to sign my name or Dad's, so I just scrawled something illegible. As I left the store, something strange happened. I felt cheerful, like actually happy, for the first time in absolute ages. So when I hit the next boutique, I went in and got a few more things to add to the Franny Ford Fall Collection: a brown skirt with soft lace trim and a shirt with embroidered flowers and a woolly sweater coat. The people at the register here were way less concerned with my credentials, accepting the card and sliding it through the register with genuine nonchalance. I hit up a couple more places and I then made my way to the subway in a far better mood than I would have thought possible when I got up that morning.

It was very dark by the time I let myself into the apartment. The lights were off in the living room, so I didn't realize Dad was there until he spoke. Or maybe "spoke" is putting it lightly. "Exploded" would be more accurate.

"*Where* have you been?" he started. "I called your cell about twenty times." He flicked the lamp on and stared at my shopping bags. "What is that? Is that what I think it is?"

"I went shopping."

"Excuse me?" His voice was all icy and emotionless, like an Arctic snow sphere.

"I went shopping," I repeated bravely.

"Jesus, Franny," he said again, getting a bit louder. "Do you have any idea what time it is? I called Rhia's house and she said she hadn't seen you since lunch but you were supposed to come over after school and didn't. What is *wrong* with you? How could you just disappear?"

"I dunno, I needed some clothes. I wanted something new."

"Great," Dad snapped. "You needed clothes. So you went, good God, Franny, to Bartolomeo? Did you use my credit card for this?" His eyes narrowed to practically reptilian slits. It was a total Voldemort look. And he would die if he knew how many wrinkles he had just made. "You did, didn't you?"

"I don't get it," I said slowly. "You and Mom can have your midlife crises and do whatever you want. You can take off for Africa or hang out with Celia or spend your life buying clothes that try too hard or are too young or just too stupid and you don't even care."

"I think we're talking about two different things."

"I think not!"

Horrified, I realized there were tears in my eyes. "I just don't see why you get to do whatever the hell you want and I can't buy a few clothes," I muttered.

"A few clothes?" He was screaming now, a real actual yell. "A few clothes! Look at those bags! This is unacceptable. Give me that credit card back. Now."

"No." Something about getting Dad to abandon his nonviolent communication mode was deeply satisfying.

Dad's face changed. "I've had enough of this. You obviously can't be trusted with the level of responsibility you've had lately."

"I didn't ask for that responsibility! I didn't ask to find my own meals and do my own laundry and fester around all alone in a dirty, abandoned apartment every day," I yelled back.

"Look," Dad began, but I almost didn't hear him.

"I hate you so much," I screamed, knowing, as I did so, that this wasn't entirely true. This small fact made me even more angry, so I repeated myself at the absolute top of my lungs. "I hate you!"

I was heading to my room to slam my door as loudly as I possibly could when I passed Zooey, who was leaning on her crutches in the hallway, lurking around like some disease or pimple that should have gone away and stopped contaminating the world by now.

"Eavesdropping?" I snapped as I passed her. "Oh, how the mighty have fallen."

chapter 17

The next morning, I was lying in bed slapping the snooze button on my alarm clock and trying to figure out if I could possibly wangle not going to school again when there was a very soft and almost timid knock on the door.

"Franny?" Dad asked. "Can I come in?"

I pretended I hadn't heard.

"OK, I'm coming in," he said.

I said nothing and rolled over to face the wall. Avoidance has always been a strong suit of mine. Dad sat down on the bed next to me.

"Hey."

Silence.

"Why don't you sit up and we can talk?"

I stared at the wall some more. My alarm, which had been on snooze, decided at exactly this moment to unsnooze itself. The noise erupted into the silent room like an emergency siren. I made no move to turn it off. After a few moments, Dad reached over and silenced it

"OK, sports fan, come on." He reached out and touched my hair. I jerked my head away, not sure of why I was being such a brat, but only knowing that now that I had started, I couldn't really stop.

"I think we both said some things yesterday that we wish we hadn't."

He was clearly back to self-help book talk. Fabulous.

"But I also think we said some things that had a grain of truth in them."

I said nothing. Why abandon a winning vein of commentary?

"Franny."

"I don't want to talk about it," I mumbled, rolling over to face him

"Why not?"

"Because there's nothing to say."

"I disagree."

Shocker.

"I am sorry, Franny, truly sorry that I haven't been around more." He stopped. "And I wish that things were a little less complicated right now, with your mom gone and Zooey hurt. It's not easy for any of us." He touched my head again, only this time I didn't jerk it away. "But the way to show that is *not* by spending a lot of money on a lot of clothes you don't really need."

"How would you know what I do and don't need?"

"Oh, give it up, Franny. In my book, no fourteen-year-old needs Bartolomeo. I didn't set foot in that store until I was forty."

"Well, Dad, what do you want me to say? You obviously waited too long." A small giggle escaped me.

"God," Dad muttered. "How did I end up with such a quarrelsome little rat?"

I sat up. "I was switched at birth. You have no idea how much my real family appreciates me."

But saying that much aloud exhausted me, so I threw myself back down on my pillow.

"Do you really hate me?" Dad asked.

"Are you really asking?" I countered.

"Yes."

"Then, yes."

We existed in semihostile silence for a few minutes.

"Is there something on your neck?" Dad asked.

I nodded. "A bandage." Dad's eyebrows rose quizzically. "Knife fight," I explained casually, then giggled as the quizzical look was replaced by one of frustration. "I actually got a henna tattoo."

"Henna?" Dad said, puzzled. I tugged the bandage down so he could see. "Not really my speed, but it's not terrible," he mused. Then, "You better get ready for school."

"I'm not going."

"Yes. You are."

Another day, another pop quiz, another lunch in the fluorescent-drenched cafeteria . . .

If I were to have a Bill Murray *Groundhog Day* experience and keep waking up on the same day over and over, I probably wouldn't even know it. My days are that identical. In fact, the only thing that distinguished this particular day was that Rhia was on a field trip to Ellis Island for her Immigration and Transformation class, which meant that I was having a little difficulty reaching my locker dial without her five feet and seven inches subtly coming to my rescue. And which Brianna Bronstein naturally had to comment on as she swept past me in a cloud of goggle-eyed first-year boys and contraband Thierry Mugler perfume (the scent of which I only recognized because Rhia's mom deemed it "too Lemon Fresh Joy" and handed her barely used bottle down to Rhia).

"Oh, look, little Frances needs a stepping stool!" she cooed.

That was so far below the belt that it was practically on the sole of my shoe. She ought to be spending a fraction of her monthly hair budget on charm school.

"Need some help?" Carter Cohen-Chang swung in beside me, happily interrupting Brianna's commentary. As he leaned his head against the wall of lockers, the navy forelock swooped across his eyebrows.

"Uh, no," I lied. "I got it." I had requested a locker change three times already, but they filled locker change requests in order of seniority. That meant I could only get a new locker after all the second-, third-, and fourth-years—who, I would like to note, have already *completed* their growth spurts—got new lockers.

"OK," Carter said agreeably. Then, he added, "Look, I've been trying to find you since the paper came out, but you've been kind of MIA. I know your article didn't make it into the paper. So," he continued, "I said something about it to River."

"You *said* something to him?" I dropped down from my tiptoes and turned to face Carter.

"Well, yeah, I mentioned it and he said you were working on it still." Carter ran his hands through the navy jet of hair. "And that seemed kind of funny, 'cause I know you said you had finished it the other day."

But I hadn't known it *stunk* the other day.

The cold, wormy, can't-think-can't-move feeling came back momentarily. Then I thawed enough to speak.

"I guess it needed more work than I thought," I said as casually as I could.

"Did River tell you that?"

"Yeah." I leaned back against my locker. "Apparently it was too opinionated and emotional and not objective." I shrugged. "I didn't realize I was doing that, but River said he couldn't print it because it wasn't journalism."

Miss Teen Antarctica was practically spilling her frozen guts.

"Can I read it?" Carter asked. I noticed there were ink stains on his uniform. Probably, he had been up all night writing various nuggets of brilliance by candlelight. Although he did seem more the MacBook than quill-pen type.

"No."

"Why not?"

"Because it *sucks*. Because River says it's unprintable and I'm going to revise it . . . maybe. But I'm certainly not going to let anyone see it the way it is now."

"The other day you were pretty happy with it," Carter said.

"The other day, River hadn't told me it stunk."

"Since when has River's opinion been the only one on the planet?"

Since *always*. Since dinosaurs walked the earth and amoebas frolicked in primordial sludge.

"He is the editor," I said cautiously.

"Can I read it?" Carter repeated.

"No," I said. Then I relented. I mean, Carter was only a second-year, but he was a good writer and had been super helpful so far. "OK, yes."

Carter leaned a bit closer to me. I noticed his eyes were very light brown, much lighter than I'd first thought, almost a tea color. I blinked. What was I doing staring into Carter Cohen-Chang's eyes?

Somehow before I could help it, words flew out of my mouth, words that I was so insecure about that I would only ever say them to my nearest and dearest, most trustworthy and beloved friends.

"Um, if I tell you the combination, would you open my locker for me?"

chapter 18

That night after my shower, I locked myself in the bathroom and played around for a while, trying to figure out what I would look like with bangs (an Afghan hound, evidently) and which hairstyle best showed off the henna neck. I started thinking that maybe who you were was connected, at least a little bit, to how you looked. Because I was an awfully wishy-washy person and, as I studied myself, I realized there was not a single feature of my appearance that wasn't wishy-washy too. Both my hair and eyes were essentially no-colored. Like, my hair was a really light brown but close enough to blond that sometimes people called it dishwater, and my eyes were the sort that look green or gray or blue, depending on the lighting or what I wore. Even the waves of my hair were neither-this-nor-that, not circular or bouncy enough to count as curly but much too defined to be straight.

I was scrupulously applying Mud Miracle to my pores when I heard Zooey crutch down the hall.

Knock. Knock.

I smoothed the green mask a bit closer to my hairline and ignored her. This was a good time to shed my wishy-washiness, make my personality more definite. I was going to be refined. Restrained. Regal, even.

"Franny, you've been in there forever."

Silent. Superior. Stately.

"I need to get in."

"Use Dad's bathroom."

"I need to get in *here*, Franny."

"I'll be just a minute." I capped Mud the Miracle and ran my fingers under the tap.

"Franny!"

"I said, *just a minute*!"

According to the *Post*, there was this Malaysian mystic who had predicted that a large asteroid was going to smash into the earth sometime in the next six months. Africa was going to ram India and ninety percent of the Atlantic Ocean would be displaced, flooding Canada and America all the way to the 105th meridian. Supposedly, it could be the end of the world as we know it.

But never mind. Zooey needed the bathroom.

I opened the door, my face swathed in moist greenness.

"God!" Zooey exclaimed, pushing past me.

"God!" I mimicked, in exactly the same tone of voice, then regretted it. I could be mature. Majestic. Modest. Back in my room, I pulled out *Her Glorious Awakening*, which was Rhia's mom's newest book. I was pretty well absorbed when I heard Zooey call out my name.

"What?" I yelled back.

I couldn't really make out her answer, so I returned to the princessa and her scoundrel lover. After a few minutes, there was a pounding on my door, and then Zooey shoved it open before I could respond.

"I need your help," she said.

"What?"

"I need, um, like a pad or a tampon or something. I don't know where you keep them. I thought they'd be in the bathroom, but they're not."

"I think there are some in there." But I rolled off my bed anyway and rummaged through the front pocket of my backpack until I found a pad.

"Here."

After Zooey crutched off, I tried to go back to my book, but I couldn't exactly concentrate in the same way. This was the first time Zooey had ever asked me for a pad, and since we shared a bathroom, I was pretty sure this was the first time she'd ever needed one. It was one of the reasons Mom worried about Zooey doing so much ballet.

Sighing, I got up off my bed and trotted down the hall to the bathroom. My Mud Miracle was all dry and itchy. I needed to wash it off anyway, I rationalized. But I sort of wasn't surprised when I got to the bathroom door and saw it was still closed.

"Can I get in? I need to wash my mask off."

"Use Dad's bathroom," Zooey shot back.

"Fine," I snapped.

"Wait." There was a pause. "I can't figure this out," she said.

The door swung open. Zooey's face was streaked with tears. "I can't believe this happened," she whispered.

"You're a woman now," I said sarcastically, then regretted it. "What can't you believe?" I asked a bit more nicely.

"This. How did I end up like this?" The tears were streaking down her face in earnest now, and her breath heaved out in huge, blubbering gasps. It reminded me of the way she had cried the night she broke her leg. Jokes about womanhood aside, these were old-sounding sobs—adult tears, not kid ones.

"Zooey, like, you know you have to get your period sometime. I've had mine for over a year now and I'm younger than you are," I pointed out.

"But I don't want it. I can't have it."

I didn't know what to say so I just said nothing, which was evidently not the right response, since Zooey decided to pull out her favorite insult for maximum effect.

"You can't understand because you're not a dancer," she spat out.

What she meant by this, of course, was, “You can’t understand because you’re not talented and special like me and all of my friends.”

“Fine,” I said, turning to leave.

“Wait,” Zooey said. She was still crying but not with the same intensity, more just a slow, quiet leaking. “Can you help me?”

“Why should I bother?” I asked honestly. “And why do you need help? This is so not a big deal.” I tossed her a clean washcloth and headed out.

chapter 19

Needless to say, I hadn't even made it the ten feet back to my bedroom before I started feeling like completely and totally awful. It wasn't just that I felt sorry for Zooey.

It was Mom.

And by Mom, I wasn't talking about My Real Mother, the Queen, or My Real Mother, the Schoolteacher in Iowa, or My Real Mother, Who Was Gracious and Sophisticated and Never Owned (Let Alone *Wore*) a Barrette Made of Little Rag People Handcrafted by Guatemalan Peasants.

No, I meant *Mom*, the cultural anthropologist who lived and breathed the East Central African coming-of-age ritual and who once actually stormed into the Stanton Health and Wellness office after reading the *Personal Blossoming* book they gave us because of its insufficient attention to certain parts of the female anatomy. Like, if I were magically to turn into an Olsen twin *and* live until the age of a hundred, I will never encounter a greater shame.

And even knowing that it could all be so much worse—because someone could be, like, painting lines on my stomach to celebrate my fertility or dumping me into the center of a lake so I could demonstrate my independence swimming home or force-feeding me red beans and corn cakes because I don't know *why*—I have to admit that when I finally did get my period (which, unlike Zooey, I actually *wanted*, because I was by that point the only girl in Health and Wellness who didn't have it), I was still extremely weirded out. And Mom was truly great. She drew me a bath and made sure I took Aleve and did not once reference the consequences of female maturation in patriarchal agrarian societies. And the next day we went to this antique store and she bought me this really, really old and beautiful hammered gold bracelet with flowers and birds carved on it.

Normally, I ached for the everyday things that had changed since Mom left—like the way we used to sit around a table eating dinner together or coming home to an apartment that felt inhabited or simply having my field trip permission slips get signed so that the principal didn't have to call Dad as we were leaving school. But as I stormed away from Zooey, I couldn't stop myself from feeling rotten because she was going to miss the *special* Momliness that should have come along with this.

I could almost feel the word *doormat* magically tattooing itself in permanent, non-henna ink on my forehead as I headed back to the bathroom.

"Zo?" I said, knocking lightly. "It's me. I'm sorry about what I said a moment ago. Are you OK?"

"Why should you bother?"

I winced as I heard my own words mimicked back at me. I tried the doorknob and realized it was open. "I'm coming in," I said, turning it more forcefully.

Inside the bathroom, Zooey was standing over the sink, rinsing out her underwear. I felt my stomach turn over a little. Mom had taken care of that for me.

"I wondered if you'd called Mom," I said.

"No." The harshness in Zooey's voice was something new, I realized. *I* was the grouchy and discontented one in the family. I wore too much black and, on occasion, too much smudged eyeliner and got in fights with Mom and Dad. She was all pink and sunny and had curls that actually bounced.

"You should tell Mom," I said. "She'll want to know."

"Only if she can shove a tape recorder in my face and interview me about it."

I giggled, partly out of nervousness, and partly from the accuracy. Because Zooey and I didn't talk to each other, we had never actually discussed Mom's going away and what it really meant. And I hadn't told her about Dad and Celia.

"Anyway, if she wanted to be here, she would," Zooey continued.

"She'll be back in the spring, maybe earlier if she gets enough research done," I parroted.

Zooey snorted. "Whatever."

She turned toward the sink and messed around with her hair for no apparent reason. I sat down on the edge of the bathtub. "Do you need anything?"

"Don't bother."

"Oh, please," I spat back before I could help myself. "Spare me the wounded bird act."

"Excuse me?" Zooey answered haughtily.

"You act all put upon, like I'm the one walking around making your life miserable. Like, what did I ever do to you?"

Zooey made a face. "Franny, you always have to make yourself the center of everything."

"Me?" I couldn't believe it. "On what planet? I am so never the middle of anything. I don't have tutus and I don't get my picture up in the subway and I don't have people worrying about my every step." I realized I was almost shaking. "I think what you hate is that for the first time in your life, you don't have ballet to make you different. You just have to live, and you have no idea how to do it."

"Shut up!" Zooey's face was white.

But now that I had started, I couldn't seem to stop. I was practically the Niagara Falls of Things You Should Think About

Before Opening Your Mouth. "You shut up! Stop bossing me around!"

Zooey was shaking also. "You don't get it. Your life is cake, Franny. Everything is so stupidly easy for you!" Her mouth twisted up a little. "You're the one who gets everything."

"Oh, right." I rolled my eyes. "*I* have everything. I am just one four-foot-ten bundle of joy and privilege." Zooey shrugged. "Oh, please. You spend most of your time ignoring me because I'm not important enough or special enough to talk to. If you hadn't broken your leg, you probably wouldn't even be talking to me now. It's just that now you're desperate." I wasn't screaming anymore.

Zooey sighed. "Unbelievable," she muttered.

"No kidding." I reached for the doorknob.

"Don't leave," she said suddenly.

I folded my arms and stared at her. "Just once, I wish you would blush," I muttered, feeling the angry flush that had automatically spread through my face while we were fighting.

Zooey sighed. "Just once, I wish you could get over yourself."

"Excuse me?" I said with as much dignity as I could muster.

Zooey shut the toilet lid and sat down. "I dunno, Franny; maybe I'm just tired of you acting like I somehow got some better deal of life."

"You kind of did," I pointed out.

"Because I'm a dancer?"

"Yes." I paused. "Because it means you never have to, like, *do* anything for yourself. Just because you have this talent and passion, you get to have your whole life taken care of. You don't even order your own take-out. And you're, you know, *gorgeous*, and . . ." I stopped, embarrassed. "You know." There was a long silence.

"It just *seems* easier," Zooey said at last. "But it's not like that at all." She ran a hand through her hair in a tired way. For the first time, I realized that she had developed a rash of pimples along her scalp line and that her typically springy curls looked limp and almost greasy. "It's not at all sorted out or settled for me. It's like I'm in a race and just when I hit the finish line, it shifts and becomes further away. Like wherever I get to is never quite good enough. I could always do better, and there's always about ten other people gaining on me. Even when I was still Juliet, it never felt like what I could do was enough.

"So I feel the same way about you, Franny, that you feel about me. It's like *you* got the better deal. Because you have real friends, and a real life, and you get to go to a school with all sorts of different people and you get the chance to figure out who it is you're going to be. And you wear crazy things, and get *lace* drawn on the back of your neck, and go to parties, and know how to be with Mom and Dad, and the three of you are the real family and I'm some Goody Two-shoes who just happens to sleep here. Like I kind of think it's cool you fight with them. I wouldn't even know how."

"Zooey," I broke in, to let her know that there wasn't like anything so magical or complicated about fighting. It just sort of *happened*, and later you regretted it. But she kept talking.

"All I'm saying, Franny, is that you have this whole identity. I'm a one-trick pony. It's just ballet for me. And it means that I don't have friends and I don't really do anything else. All I have are people I compete with. So, yeah, I love dancing, and I'm glad I can do it. But sometimes I wish I could be more like you."

chapter 20

You can say the grass is always greener. You can tell me that still waters run deep. You can even go so far as to spout on about all that glitters or how there's more than meets the eye. But let me just say that up until Zooey decided to go all *Are You There God? It's Me, Margaret*, it would have been awfully hard to convince me that spending time with my sister could produce any emotions outside the continuum from dull to dreadful. But it was just a few days later that I was in my bedroom, being bored to a pulp by *The Yearling* (the latest offering from the ninth grade curriculum in the People Are Less Worthy Than Animals category) when Zooey banged on my door and pretty much demanded that I stop working and entertain her.

"Ah, yes," I said, sitting up. "You can take the ballerina off the stage, but you can't take the prima out of the ballerina."

"Well, I'm *bored*," she moaned, sticking an unbent coat hanger down into her cast and rooting around like Julia Child whipping meringue. Talk about begging for a case of tetanus. "Why is Dad never home?"

"That looks like a really bad idea," I said, ignoring her question and gesturing to the coat hanger. "I know a broken leg is bad and all, but don't you think a *gangrenous* leg would be a lot worse?"

"But my leg is all itchy!" Slowly, she braced her hand on my night table to lower herself to the floor. "Anyway, seriously, why is Dad, like, never here? Has it just been since Mom went away? Or was it always like this and I never knew 'cause I always had ballet?" She jammed the coat hanger farther down into her cast. I stared at the floor and thought about Celia and her three-foot-high suction boots.

Aloud, I hedged, "Well, even before Mom left, Dad didn't get home right at five." Zooey stared at me. "But yeah, it's different now," I admitted.

Zooey leaned onto her back and raised her unbroken leg into the air and began pointing and flexing her foot in a series of rhythmic half circles.

"I don't see why she had to go away," Zooey sighed. She began kicking her straightened leg down to the floor, then back up in the air, like a guillotine blade.

"She had to do her research," I said.

"Do you think that's really it?" Zooey paused with her leg midair and made a quick little flourish with her toes, the way anyone else would make a hand gesture.

I hugged my knees in to my chest. "When I was, um, in Dad's store last week?" I said. It came out questioningly, very timid. Zooey's foot tapped the air encouragingly. "There was this woman there," I continued.

"Like what kind of woman?"

"Like the glamorous sort. Like someone who would wear clothing made from peacock feathers. Her name was Celia."

"There was a woman named Celia in Dad's store?" The foot planted on the ground.

"Well, she works there."

"Oh." The foot went back in the air.

"Dad smiled at her," I added.

"So?"

I didn't say anything.

"So, why are you telling me that Dad smiled at some woman who works for him?"

"It was the *way* he smiled at her," I specified.

"Way was how?"

"All crinkly."

"Crinkly?" Zooey said dubiously. I sighed.

"He smiled at her like maybe he was having an affair with her," I blurted.

The foot stopped midair.

"Are you serious?" Zooey said.

"Yes," I emphasized. Zooey smashed her lips together. "I probably overreacted," I added.

"Maybe not." Zooey kicked her foot into the air again, rather violently. "I'm so mad Mom left," Zooey said.

Something about how easily she was able to say that kind of killed me.

"I mean, *you're* the one who always got in all those bad fights with her," she continued.

That was true. Before Mom left, it had seemed like I was always running to my room and slamming the door over something (or *nothing*) that she had said.

"But," she continued, "now whenever I talk to her, I have to keep myself from starting to scream." She stopped, then added, "She didn't even come when I got hurt."

We were quiet for a while. Staring at Zooey's toes reminded me that my own were in a sad state. I leaned over and pulled a bottle of polish off the floor, where it had fallen between my nightstand and bed. Slowly, I started touching up my nails.

Zooey watched me for a minute, then asked, "What color is that?" It was a very dark blue, so dark it almost looked black.

"Corpse," I managed with a straight face.

"For real?" Zooey asked.

I lifted the bottle up so I could look at the label. "It's, uh, Magical Midnight." I flipped the bottle right side up and dunked just the tip of the brush into the bottle. In my endless quest for a less amateurish pedicure, I was working on a less-polish, smoother-stroke strategy.

"So," she said, "what do you think we should do about Dad and Celia?"

"What do you mean, what should we do?" I asked.

"You know," Zooey shrugged.

"No, *Parent Trap* Girl, I don't," I answered.

Zooey giggled. "I *was* thinking something like that." She tried to roll over onto her stomach, but her cast was too big, so she curled over on her side. "Well, we don't know anything for sure. I'm reserving judgment till I meet this woman."

"Yeah," I agreed, already feeling better just that someone besides me knew about this.

"If you're right, I don't quite know what to do." She bit her lip. "But I think we need to go investigate. Pay them a surprise visit and get some more info."

An image of Dad and Celia holding hands over a copy of *GQ* flitted through my mind. I winced. "You mean go now?"

"Why not?" Zooey smiled a tense smile.

"We can't."

"Why not?" Zooey repeated.

Because I didn't want to know more than I already did.

On the other hand, it was kind of nice to have someone else involved, and I probably was being silly and inventing stuff instead of paying attention to facts.

"OK."

"Good." Zooey nodded coolly. "So what should I wear?"

"What do you *wear*?" I repeated. Did Joan of Arc ask what she should wear to the *stake*?

"I'll just feel more prepared if I'm wearing a costume," Zooey explained, lurching over to my closet and pulling down my rhinestone hoodie.

"That's not a costume," I snickered. "That's what Rhia's mom gave me for my birthday last year."

Undeterred, Zooey ran a hand over my dresser, holding up my eyeliner. "And can I borrow this also?"

"Don't you think you're going overboard?" I said. "We're just going to spy on Dad a little."

Zooey drew herself up until she stood beautifully straight. "Finding out about Celia is a performance like any other in my life."

chapter 21

When the best-laid plans go awry, no one ever tells you it's because of *makeup*. I am the last person to talk about a need to limit eyeliner. But by the time Zooey and I got done primping for our Great Adventure and made it down to the store, the lights were already off and the "Closed" sign was hanging. I groaned. Holmes and Watson never failed to nab their man because they spent too long adjusting their deerstalker hats.

"Crud," Zooey said, pounding on the window.

"No one's here," I said, wrinkling my nose. "We're too late."

"We don't know that," Zooey said, leaning on the doorbell.

"This is *Dad*," I said. Pulling out my cell phone, I texted him. A few seconds later, he came to the front of the store.

"Girls?" he questioned, unlocking the door to let us in.

"Hi," Zooey said cheerfully. "We missed you. Time to come visit. So, are you all alone here?"

A brilliant time to discover Zooey had all the subtlety of a freight train.

"Hi, Daddy." I breezed past him. "We just missed you."

"Surprise visits twice in one week?" Dad questioned.

"I know," I said, shaking my head. "Lucky you."

"Awfully quiet in here," Zooey mused, hopping to the center of the room. "Is there anyone here but us?"

Apparently the more talented your feet are, the more ways there are to put them in your mouth.

"I think what Zooey means is that we haven't seen you in, oh, *forever*, and we'd love to have dinner," I backpedaled.

"Sounds fun, but I have an event I've promised to get to. A designer is holding a show in her studio."

"Oh," I wheedled, "that sounds missable."

Dad shrugged. "Possibly."

"Maybe Celia could go for you?"

I felt bold saying her name aloud.

"How do you know about Celia?" Dad said. He sounded genuinely surprised. Aha! A clue. He was being evasive about Celia. I raised my eyebrows at Zooey.

Aloud, I said bluntly, "I met her and her thigh-high boots the other day."

"That's right." Dad remembered. "There's been so much going on since then that I just forgot." He looked at me. "I guess those are some boots."

"They probably wouldn't do well in combat," I agreed, trying to figure out if we were doing banter or detective work.

"Well, Celia's gone home already," Dad said. "But I have a better idea. Why don't you guys come with me? We'll pop into the show for a little while and then go out for dinner."

"Us?" Zooey asked.

"Can we go to dinner in Chinatown?" I bargained. Dad *hated* Chinatown. Knockoff purses gave him panic attacks.

"If you insist."

So much for detective work. There were no manuals on culprits willing to buy you bottomless bowls of wonton soup.

"I insist."

Dad, very occasionally, had hosted events for designers at his store, and Zooey and I generally went to them. They tended to be filled with friends of the designer (all wearing black-rimmed glasses and cartilage studs and jeans) and "catered" by friends of the designer (meaning homemade hummus). Dad would be happy and excited, and then later, he and Mom would stay up all night talking about the problems with supporting designers whose talents didn't match current taste demands.

What that usually meant was that he hadn't sold what he'd wanted to.

This event was nothing like that. It wasn't just that there were strobe lights and posturing models stalking down an actual runway along one side of the room. It was also that you could have put an eighteen-hole golf course inside the studio and had room left over. The brie puffs were probably the best thing I'd had to eat in the past year. The crowd was very see-and-be-seen, with a lot of drawling and air kissing. It sort of reminded me of the Stanton cafeteria at lunch, minus plastic trays.

As Dad circled the room, Zooey looked at me.

"So Celia wasn't at the store," she said.

"Yeah," I agreed.

"And she's not here either." Zooey frowned. "Does that mean anything? Like, something good?"

"I dunno." I reached for another brie puff.

"Well, do you mind if we find a place to sit?" Zooey asked. "My leg is feeling like Jell-O."

I glanced around the packed, minimalist, furnitureless room and made a face. "How about there?" I asked, gesturing to the back corner. There weren't any chairs, but we could sit on the floor and lean against the wall.

Zooey looked dubiously at the corner. "I guess there's nowhere else," she agreed.

A few minutes later, as we painfully squeezed through the crowds, I began to regret choosing a corner that was so far away. I opened my mouth to ask Zooey if we should just go ahead and ask Dad to leave when I realized she wasn't behind me.

Lost: one sister. Age: sixteen. Feet: impressive. Mouth: open too often.

I flipped around and started retracing the path back to where Zooey had been. Halfway there, I felt a small tug on my arm.

"Franny?" It was Carter, still wearing his school uniform and looking really bored.

"What are you doing here?" I asked, surprised.

"This is my mom's show. She makes clothes." He brushed his hair out of his eyes. "Why are *you* here?"

"My dad had an invite and it's kind of a long story." I looked up at him. "I thought everyone at Stanton except for me and Rhia had boring businessy parents."

Carter laughed. "My dad is a boring businessperson. My mom is . . ." He scanned the room. "There." He pointed to a small, unsmiling woman wearing a dress that would not have looked out of place in the nineteenth century. There were serious hoop-skirts involved.

"Not boring," I agreed.

"No," Carter said, reaching for a brie puff. "And she hates these sort of things. She only does them because she needs people to see her stuff. But it's kind of nice you're here." He stopped. "I was actually thinking about you. I just finished reading your article."

Oh.

"It's so obvious," Carter continued. "I mean, of course, River couldn't print it as news."

"So he told me." It came out a little curt.

"Hey, relax," Carter drawled. "So you're not a news journalist, Franny. Big deal. I think maybe you're a *columnist*."

"Huh?"

"You know," Carter said impatiently. "You tell things like you see them, and maybe that's the way it is and maybe that's the way it isn't, but it's OK to have it be your perspective, and what gets people to read it is the personality of the voice." He shrugged. "I can't believe River missed it. We've been talking forever about how we need a new columnist."

"He didn't miss it," I defended. "He said all that stuff you said about the personality and opinion."

"But he thought you had to change it to be like everything else we already have, and I don't. I say we take what you're good at, and that's it."

I thought about it. "But isn't River right? I mean, if I'm not being a journalist . . ." I trailed off.

Carter sighed. "Look, for most people, writing a column is a heck of a lot harder to do than just reporting facts. You happen to be able to do it automatically. It's just, you know, who you are." He squeezed my shoulder. "I gotta go. My mom is waving at me. But I have a movie review that I need a staffer to write up. You want to try it?"

"OK."

"Great. I'll give you the details at school."

"Who was that?" Zooey asked, materializing beside me. "He looks cool. Is he as cool as he looks?"

I turned to her. "Elementary, my dear Watson."

chapter 22

It's funny. When there is a Malaysian mystic predicting the destruction of the world, it gets buried on page three billion of the *Post.* When RIVER MCGEE AND BRIANNA BRONSTEIN BREAK UP, there is actual pandemonium throughout the halls of E. C. Stanton.

"Jenny Wong said it was because he discovered that she had breast implants," Caroline Abbott confided, leaning across the library table.

Rhia and I gasped reflexively.

"And," Caroline continued juicily, "it turned out they were made out of this artificial plasma stuff that is totally petroleum-based. And you know how much River cares about the environment. He said he couldn't believe she would pollute her body like that and from now on he wouldn't be able to look at her without feeling tainted himself."

Rhia and I sighed at the magnificence of this. My own chest may have been virtually nonexistent, but it was at least one hundred percent organic.

"Anyway," Caroline said, slinging her books upward, "I have to run." She winked at us. "Toodles, ladies."

"Toodles," I echoed, envisioning a heartbroken River waiting to be consoled. "Right in time for Halloween," I added to Rhia.

"Now we really have to figure out our costumes," she answered.

We'd been trying to come up with the perfect costume idea for the past week. Since neither of us managed any significant brainstorms between study hall and the end of the day, Rhia came over after school.

"Maybe I should go as an actual river," I mused, pawing aimlessly through a large bag of fake blood and fangs and other Halloween props. "You know, as a declaration of my love. With a wreath of glow-stick boats in my hair."

"I think we need to figure out what type of costumes we want. Do we want to be gory or funny or romantic or what?" Rhia asked, fingering a pack of fake tattoos speculatively.

We'd been inspirationless for maybe a half an hour when Zooey limped in, her crutch signaling her arrival with loud advance thumps, like a drummer in a marching band.

"Hey," she said. "I thought I heard something."

"Hi," I said, glancing at Rhia. I hadn't told her how much better Zooey and I were getting along now. It was like Zooey was home-world and Rhia was school-world, and I wasn't sure how I felt about them meeting. "We're trying to figure out our Halloween costumes."

"I forgot Halloween was coming." Zooey wrinkled her nose. "I've lost all track of time just hanging around the apartment doing nothing but physical therapy exercises and boring tutoring assignments." She sat down on this old trunk that we keep pushed against one side of the couch. "What are you going to be?"

"We have *no* idea," Rhia moaned. "But there's this big carnival at school, with a haunted house."

"Really, a haunted language-arts wing," I corrected her.

"And they're hiring carriages for hayrides in the park and stuff," Rhia added. "And unless we can figure something out, we're going to have to go in our uniforms."

"Can I help?" Zooey asked.

"I doubt it," I said, a little more firmly than I'd intended.

There was a pause. "OK," Zooey answered. "It's just I happen to have, you know, a whole lot of costumes."

Rhia looked at me. "Like ballet costumes?" she asked. "I don't know that we're the tutu types."

"It's all kinds of stuff," she said. "Not everything is a tutu."

"You wouldn't mind?" Rhia asked.

"They're just sitting in my closet." She leaned her hands heavily on the edge of the trunk for balance, wobbling slightly as she got up. "Do you want to see?"

We followed her to her seriously pink bedroom, where she threw open the doors of the wardrobe Mom had gotten for her costumes once they stopped fitting in the closet. A froth of spangles exploded out at us. The floor of the wardrobe was layered thickly with toe shoes so worn that they were now gray, and the back of the door was obscured by a cascade of ribbons and tiaras.

"Wow," Rhia said unnecessarily. "I guess you do have a lot of costumes."

Zooey began tugging various items out. "Milkmaid?" she asked, tossing down a peasant dress with a bodice. "Red Riding Hood?" She added a short crimson cape. "Harem girl?" She smirked, fluttering a pair of wide pants and spangled bikini top.

"What is *that* from?" Rhia gasped.

"Oh, I was in the dream sequence from *Le Corsaire* two years ago," Zooey said, rummaging through the accessories. "Look, here's the headpiece," she added, holding out a sequined headband with a big blue feather. "And there's a flapper dress, from this jazz-age thing I did last year. Remember, Franny?"

I did. I'd had a fight with Mom in the taxi on the way there over something so stupid that I couldn't even remember, and spent most of the recital biting the inside of my cheek in anger. I had a big blister by the end of the show.

"Of course, there *are* tutus, should you feel like a classical moment." She heaped a pile of sparkling white into my arms, the masses of the fragile skirt filling my arms completely. I fingered the satin bodice speculatively, wondering what it would be like to wear something so delicate. "And here's pink, if you feel like doing the Dance of the Flowers." A swell of rose landed on top of the white. "Oh, and look. This was my first tutu," she said, holding out a tiny dress.

We made appropriate *awwwww* noises. "What about this gold one?" Rhia said, reaching her hand out to touch the skirt. "That's pretty."

Zooey and I looked at each other for a moment. I remembered her standing on the stage at Lincoln Center, curtsying deeply, the golden coronet in her hair, the huge smile on her face visible even rows and rows back from the stage.

"That's from my last recital," she said at last. "The one where Arturo Peretti saw me dance and asked me to audition to be Juliet."

There was a strained pause.

"It's OK. You didn't know. Here, look," she changed the topic. "Here's a Harlequin dress. This would fit you, Franny."

"OK." Quickly, I slipped into the boldly patterned satin. Rhia and Zooey burst out laughing.

"You look *great*," Rhia squealed.

I turned toward the mirror, pleating the skirt with my hands as I smoothed it down.

"I remember you wearing this," I said, feeling vaguely imposterish. Unlike Zooey, I never made it to the recital stage in ballet, quitting after only a month because the other girls were loud and the exercises hurt my knees.

"Yeah, in *The Nutcracker*," Zooey added. "I totally hated that dance. *Turn-out, ladies*," she squawked, in a heavily accented voice. "Here's the hat." She toppled a checkered cone onto my head.

"What about me?" Rhia asked. "Can I try the flapper dress?"

"Of course!" Zooey answered. "And someone should try on Red Riding Hood."

We dove into the piles of clothing, tossing dresses back and forth to each other, giggling with each new outfit. Zooey settled onto the floor to watch us.

"So is this carnival a big deal?' she asked.

"Kind of," Rhia said, struggling to zip a pale blue fluff of a dress. "Jeez, you're tiny," she added, giving up and switching it out for a yellow one. "It's not the prom," she qualified. "But it's the only thing that'll happen until winter—school-sponsored, anyway. There's, like, other stuff that'll happen. Parties or whatever."

"Like Carter wants to have a skating party once it gets cold enough," I threw in, looking over at Zooey, quietly raking her hands through the carpet in a circular pattern. "And this girl on newspaper is going to have an insane sweet sixteen."

"And my mom said we need to figure out what play we want to see this year," Rhia said. "She always takes us out over Thanksgiving break," she explained to Zooey.

"So there's a lot going on," Zooey said at last.

I was about to toss back the automatic reply that we really had absolutely no life, but I stopped.

"Yeah," I said instead. "I guess there always does seem to be something happening." Thoughtfully, I sat back and watched Rhia, a tiara on her head, sucking in her cheeks and staring at her reflection from a number of angles.

"Zo, would you want to come to the carnival with us?" I said, shocking myself with the words. The tiara clattered to the vanity as Rhia whipped around to give me a stunned look. Her mouth opened slightly, like a burbling fish, as though she might be on the verge of saying something but was working hard not to. Zooey didn't seem to notice her reaction.

"Are you *serious*?" she bubbled ecstatically. "Like, for real? I'd *love* to. I mean, it's like a real high school event and everything."

"Don't get your hopes too high," I cut in. "It won't be that exciting."

"No, I know," Zooey backtracked. "But, wow, thanks, Franny. Are you sure you don't mind? I've never been to a real party and, anyway, I'm so sick of just being in the apartment and going nowhere but physical therapy, and I'd love to go, really."

"OK," I said, still not sure why I'd invited Zooey. It's not that I wanted her to be all mopey and miserable, but a small, mean part of me suddenly wished I could take the invite back.

"Well, these are pretty," Rhia said, sloppily pirouetting in a white dress. "Just not very Halloweeny. And I still can't zip any of them."

Zooey stared at her for a minute, then rummaged through the bag of Halloween props, pulling out a vial of fake blood. She ripped the capsule open, stood up effortfully, and sloshed the blood down Rhia's front, staining the glittering white in large crimson blotches. Rhia gasped.

"Zooey!"

"Think Bride of Frankenstein," she said, smearing a streak of blood onto Rhia's shocked cheek. "Come on, I have so many costumes; don't look at me like that!" She grabbed a pair of scissors from her desk and began slashing the net skirt into great ragged shreds. Rhia giggled nervously. "Shake your hair out," Zooey commanded. "No, more, get crazy." Rhia headbanged obligingly. "Let's find a tiara, and some cobwebs."

Zooey looked so silly and so fired up at the same time, breaking the tiara into pieces, her hands covered in fake blood, that a gurgle escaped me. It was like she was the old, adventurous, pre-ballet Zooey. I flopped onto her bed and laughed.

"Watch out," she said happily, weaving a black ribbon through the holes she had made in the tattered back of the dress, so that it laced up in a bedraggled way and fit Rhia perfectly. "You're next. Remember, I have a lot of costumes."

chapter 23

So I had some news for Linus van Pelt: *I*, Franny Ford, somehow was apparently the Great Pumpkin. Like maybe I could pull off a daily masquerade as an average kid, but by the time Halloween rolled around, yours truly was overtaken by extreme pumpkinness.

The night started out wrong, with my parents suddenly unified in an overprotective front. I swear they hadn't talked in two weeks, but the word *party* was an immediate cue for them to get Transatlantic Protect and Defend on us. Or, more accurately, on Zooey, since of course, no one was particularly concerned with my safety. But the thought of Zooey at a party made them palpitate. It was like she was actually one of those tiny plastic ballerinas forever sheltered inside a music box.

Well, it was long past time to dump her out into the thrift store of real life.

"We'll take cabs," I explained into the phone for maybe the third time, as patiently as I could. "Everywhere," I added, readjusting the skirt of my blood-drenched Sugarplum Frankenfairy tutu. "Even if it's within walking distance."

"Franny, it's not the cabs I worry about." Mom fretted through the static. "It's your sister *in her cast* at a large, crowded, and probably very dark haunted house. You know how hard she's worked at physical therapy. Really, what were you thinking when you suggested this?"

Like it was somehow *my* fault Zooey had chosen to spend her entire life to date closeted in a chalky dance studio obsessed with her hip socket.

"I'll put Zooey on," I said, marching the cordless down to her room. "She can talk for herself."

A few seconds later, I heard her yell, "Why are you trying to ruin my life?"

A small smile escaped me. At long last: the perfectly restrained Zooey loses it.

"How do you stand it?" she moaned in the taxi, once we finally managed an escape, promising to call Dad if we needed anything. "They're the worst."

"Weren't you the freak show who wanted to be like a normal teenager?" I answered breezily, glad to be the one who had avoided a fight. "Look on the bright side. Your wish came true."

Zooey shuddered. She was wearing the harem outfit because the bagginess of the pants had made it easy to disguise her cast. But I could practically see a tiara materializing on her head as she spoke.

"Well, I didn't know it was going to be like *that*!"

I couldn't help it. I leaned my head against the back of the seat and laughed.

Because Stanton has separate upper and lower schools, I'd never gone to the Halloween carnival before, just to the lower school party, which involves a lot of bobbing for apples and dart throwing in the cafeteria. It was never boring, but it was also *not* arriving at school to find the white stone façade strobed purple and orange by a row of black lights planted on the sidewalk, security guards with walkie-talkies parading in front, and horse-drawn carriages heaped with hay and pumpkins waiting resplendently at the end of the block, facing Fifth Avenue.

"Wow," I said, leaning my head out the window as we pulled

up. I had worried that Zooey might be overexcited about this party and that it wouldn't live up to her expectations. Clearly, I had wasted brainpower.

"It's like a movie," Zooey breathed.

"It's like the *Oscars*," Rhia corrected.

Zooey had never set foot in Stanton—or in any normal high school—before but whatever quality she had that drew people to her was every bit as evident in the cobwebbed halls of Stanton as it was onstage. She was like Snow White, only instead of a flock of doting bluebirds, a posse of Stanton's Most Everything collected at her fingertips.

"I suppose the harem girl costume doesn't hurt," Rhia muttered to me as we sipped hot cider on the periphery of Zooey's mass of admirers, the fake blood from our faces flaking slightly into the cups.

"And that disgustingly perfect ballet body," I added, scanning the room futilely for the newly single River McGee.

I was really working on not being jealous of Zooey. But I'd have to be a very nonobservant person not to notice that it had taken less than ten minutes of Zooey lingering in her sequined bra before Curt Marino, who was first-year class president and who had never said ONE WORD to me, appeared at my elbow. With his eyes glued to Zooey's bejeweled belly button, he asked me if we were in English together. When I stammered yes, he very unsubtly continued by asking Zooey's belly button what period she had English, which of course turned into a discussion of how Zooey had never set foot in a real high school before.

Then, because Elton Garland has never forgiven Curt for hooking up with his ex-girlfriend Violet Hirst, he had to come over. Then Violet, who reportedly has never really gotten over being ignored by Curt, came over, and Violet happens to be friends with Carmina Elliott . . .

And *voila*! *Zooey est arrivée!*

Luckily, I was able to ignore most of what happened from this point on by going with Carter to wander through the haunted language-arts wing. There was a fog machine, so we walked knee-deep through strangely glowing mist. It wasn't scary, exactly, but it did manage to be surprisingly eerie.

"This reminds me of this really old movie," Carter said, "about this fog that kills people and—"

"It turns out that the fog is made up of these ghosts," I interrupted.

"Totally!" Carter exclaimed. "They were these lepers who were murdered a hundred years before and they want revenge."

Carter Cohen-Chang watched bad TNT reruns? Shouldn't someone with navy hair and a pierced ear have more exciting pastimes?

"I can't believe you know that movie," I said honestly.

"Watched it twice," Carter confessed. "I have a kind of addiction for old horror movies."

Oh, happiness.

Within a few minutes, Carter and I were besting each other with obscure movie knowledge. His Stephen King knowledge was sadly deficient, but he knew a surprising amount about *Dracula* and lots and lots about *The Thing*, which I'd never even seen. Or heard of.

"You know, the Angelika is showing *Frankenstein* all weekend," he said casually, brushing aside a curtain of cobwebs so we could make our way from the long hallway into Ms. Hurley's classroom, appropriately enough redecorated as a graveyard. "You interested?"

Was I interested? And, more important, was this, um, a *date*?

"The original *Frankenstein* or the remake?" I asked, flicking away a plastic bat that had dropped from the ceiling.

"Please," Carter said. "You obviously haven't heard my opinions on remakes."

His opinions on remakes? What about mine? But before I could open my mouth, another plastic bat fell onto my shoulder.

"Ahh!" I shuddered. Then, suddenly, a whole avalanche of bats rained down on us, at which point I totally couldn't help it and shrieked in what could only be described as a monumentally sissy way.

"Get these off me," I cried, flailing my hands in the air.

Carter leaned forward and brushed the bats from my head. The classroom was cold, but there was this strangely warm feeling in my hair, where his hand had lingered for a split second longer than was strictly necessary. It was—I was sure—exactly the sort of tingly blaze that had come over the Contessa Elisabetta Sophia da Fiorenza in *The Contessa's Pet Rogue*, when Paco helped her stand back up after she had been bucked off by an unbroken stallion. I looked very closely at Carter, who was wearing some sort of punk-esque costume and had managed to transform his longish, barely-dress-code-compliant silky dark hair into short red spikes.

Automatically, I moved a little closer to him, to take full advantage of what was clearly a Tender Moment.

"God!" a voice screamed suddenly. "Ahhh!"

A girl I didn't know, dressed like a police officer, tore through the cobwebby door of the classroom. "Get away from me!" she yelled behind her. A guy followed, laughing, pelting her with Silly String.

"Chicken," he bawked.

I looked at Carter, who had stopped being Paco-ish and Tender

Moment–ish and suddenly looked like himself only with a bad wig. "Maybe we should get out of here," I said.

A new shower of plastic bats exploded from the ceiling. The girl shrieked.

Carter pushed aside the cobwebs.

"Definitely."

chapter 24

How could my Tender Moment be interrupted? It was so completely and totally not acceptable. After all, the contessa's first interaction with Paco went on for pages and pages. And I'm sorry: Would squealing teenagers have felled Brad and Angelina? Or Rhett and Scarlett? Even *Liesl* managed to make it through an act-of-God torrential downpour to cavort with her Nazi weasel. In fact, the absolute only couple I could think of who had their Tender Moments rudely interrupted were Romeo and Juliet. And we all know how *that* ended up.

Besides, once a Tender Moment is ruined, it's really hard to reclaim the tingly glow, I realized, as Carter and I made our way down the strobe-lit stairs and through the crowded halls. Of course, I hadn't had many Tender Moments, unless you counted four weeks last summer with David Feldman, when he was visiting his grandmother in apartment 5-K. But even though I cried when David left to go home to Buffalo, I sort of forgot about him in all of the drama of Mom moving to Kenya.

An important fact about me was that David was the only person I had ever kissed.

This meant that I was so freaking behind everyone else that I was practically the Forrest Gump of Teen Romance.

Anyway, making my way back into the front entryway of the school could have been intimidating if Carter weren't beside me, my tutu brushing up against his plaid-and-pleather-clad side. The massive foyer teemed with carnival booths and kids in all kinds of costumes. I caught a clear glimpse of Brianna Bronstein dressed in a skintight devil outfit. At the risk of being completely unfaithful to my feminist upbringing, I have to say that if I could look like that, I would wear red latex and horns every single second of my existence.

Instead, I just looked up at Carter's nice tea-colored eyes and said, "It's really crowded here."

"Well, we could get out of here and go for a hayride," he answered, sounding a bit more tentative than usual.

A hayride in an actual carriage through Central Park on Halloween with an actual male? Especially one with an ironic navy streak in his black hair which, really, truly made him look like a longer-haired, somewhat less musclely version of Superman?

"Sure."

But then something funny happened. As we made our way toward the front door of the school, I realized I wasn't sure I was ready to go on a hayride with Carter. Because if I did, it would mean I *wasn't* going to go on a hayride with River. And that was funny, because I liked Carter. I really liked Carter.

Only I *loved* River. I loved him from the very first moment I walked into the newspaper staff room the first week of school. I loved him the way I loved mushrooms on my pizza or the color black or drinking my drinks without ice—like it was an element of my personality so deeply rooted that I couldn't imagine it not being there.

And now River had finally recovered from whatever romantic amnesia had kept him blinded by Brianna, just when I was starting to feel more confident about talking to him. And when we were in a carriage, surrounded by hay, it would be so easy for him to be taken in by the moonlight glinting off my hair. . . .

I had no choice but to stop walking. Carter stopped alongside me. "I should check on my sister," I told him, surprising myself with the words. "Just to be sure she's OK."

Carter looked taken aback, but all he said was, "You have a sister?"

"Oh, yeah." Quickly, I explained about Zooey. "She's obviously more than fine, but I probably should let her know where I'm going, just because she can't walk, really."

I was using my sister as an excuse to delay going on a hayride with a cute guy. If I were to tag along with the devil (aka Brianna) as she returned to hell, I was a hundred percent certain I'd find the whole place frozen over.

But I still couldn't make myself go out that door.

Instead, with Carter tagging behind me, I squirmed through the crowded foyer, getting many a "Hey, watch it!" as we weaved through the crowds. It took about ten minutes before I realized Zooey wasn't there, so I moved into the cafeteria. Futilely, I scanned the carnival booths.

"She can't walk; she can't have gone anywhere," I fretted, suddenly forgetting about the hayride and furious at myself for deserting her. Stanton kids were so unpredictable, so wild. *Anything* could have happened to her. Zooey may have been older than I was, but she was way less jaded and experienced about things. Her idea of drugs was prescription diet pills, and while I may have been pretty disconnected from that scene at Stanton, it wasn't like I didn't know it existed. Zooey, on the other hand, was the emotional equivalent of that kid in *Flowers for Algernon*, which we'd read in school last year. He had a really low IQ and then had an operation to make him smarter and suddenly could finally experience life like everyone else.

And then, of course, he *died*.

"I'm sure Zooey is fine," Carter said reasonably. "She probably just went to sit down somewhere."

"She's crippled," I snapped. "And she's never been to a party before." I pulled out my phone and called Zooey's cell, but there was no answer.

"My parents are going to kill me if anything happens to her," I moaned. "They were upset that I even *thought* of bringing her."

Carter paused. "Hey, I'm sure it's OK."

He obviously had never met my parents. Lord Voldemort would hold less of a grudge.

Scanning the crowds, I spotted Rhia in line for a candy apple. "Have you seen Zooey?" I marched over to her. "She seemed more than fine on her own so I went up to the haunted house and now I can't find her!"

Rhia's face changed slightly. "Yeah, I saw her going outside."

"Outside? You mean, she left without me?"

"No, um, I think maybe she went on a hayride. I think she's fine."

Zooey went on a hayride? "Oh, OK." I rolled my eyes. "Well, Curt Marino *was* pretty into her."

"Yeah," Rhia said. She had a strange look on her face.

Carter gave me a small smile. "If Zooey can go for a hayride, maybe we can as well?"

I thought about it. Probably it would inspire River's jealousy to see me nestled with another guy among bales of hay in a carriage.

What was WRONG with me? Since when had I morphed into a shallow two-timer with the moral fiber of a dust mite?

"OK," I said, attempting to banish all thoughts of River.

Slowly, we made our way through the raucous crowd and out the strobe-lit front door. There was a line for the hayrides, and we joined the end of it. *Carter*, I emphasized to myself. *Carter*, who liked my writing. *Carter*, who had the warmest, most amberish eyes I'd ever seen.

I looked up to gaze into them, feeling a small tingle beginning again.

Phew. A pre-hayride Tender Moment, just when I needed it most. Boldly, I reached for Carter's hand, feeling it lock tightly into my own, as neat-fitting as a puzzle piece. We were almost to the front of the line. My heart began to throb, just the tiniest bit, as a carriage rolled toward us, returning from the park. Slowly, the horses clattered to the curb. I could hear the sounds of laughter from within the cab.

"Nooo, come on," a female voice squealed.

"Dude, can't we go again?" a familiar voice drawled to the driver. "I'll make it worth your while."

And then, before my horrified eyes, from the shadowy, romantic depths of the carriage, River emerged. There was a cocky bandanna holding back his flop of hair, eye patch dangled around his neck and grazed the top of his open-necked pirate shirt. He looked so naturally swashbuckling that I froze.

River was on a hayride? With someone else? He couldn't be back with Brianna; I had just seen her. How could someone have weaseled into my rightful place so quickly? Horrified, I watched as River held his hand down to the girl inside the carriage, smiling sweetly down toward her.

Another giggle, another squeal.

And then, I could see her, struggling to stand, grabbing his hand for balance, a huge smile on her face, sequined headband askew, metallic bikini top capping off an expanse of smooth, muscular abs.

Zooey.

chapter 25

If my life were (literally) a horror movie and I could get some mad scientist to excise scenes from my memory permanently, this is what I'd want gone, forever:

1) The delighted look on Zooey's face as she spotted me waiting in the hayride line
2) The casual way River clapped me on the shoulder, saying, "Dude, I didn't know you had a sister." *Dude!* He actually *duded* me!
3) The obvious reddening flush I could feel burning my face and arms
4) The numbing hayride that followed, me sitting frozenly beside Carter, his arm heavy across my shoulder, my mind whirling with betrayal and anger

I was quiet on the cab ride home, smashing my lips together in an effort to keep the tears hovering in my eyes from spilling over. I just couldn't think of what to say. Zooey, typically, failed to notice. That meant that I got to listen to her drool on about how amazing the carnival was, how amazing River was, how they had a date for tomorrow night. . . .

In England, they used to punish traitors by literally cutting them into four pieces. In my book, that would be a fate far too generous for Zooey Ford.

"Glad you enjoyed yourself, because that's the last time I bring you anywhere," I muttered under my breath as the cab stopped in front of our building.

"*What?*" Zooey asked.

I didn't answer, just paid the driver and stormed toward the door of the building, remembering but not caring that Zooey couldn't get in and out of cars very well. If she were to fall flat on her perfect ski-slope nose, I would—in no way, shape, or form—be able to stop a self-satisfied thrill of redemption running through me.

If I were especially lucky, she'd break the other leg.

"Franny!" she called after me, but I ignored her.

She caught up with me in the lobby, while I was waiting for the elevator.

"Franny, what is going on?"

I didn't say anything. Silence, presumably, being golden and all that.

"What's going on?" she repeated.

The elevator came just then. I stepped inside and maturely attempted to hit the door-close button before Zooey got in. But she stuck her crutch into the door in time, so it reopened.

"Franny, what's wrong with you?" she said, once she was safely inside.

"What's wrong with me?" I gasped. "What's wrong with *you*? I can't believe you!" I realized, belatedly, that I was screaming.

"What did I do?" Zooey asked.

"I can't believe you don't know," I shot back, more quietly. The elevator stopped at our floor. I got out and started walking toward our apartment door.

"Franny, I don't know what I did," Zooey pleaded from behind me. "I thought you wanted me to come. I thought you were OK with me being there. Did I not spend enough time with you?"

"Yeah, that's one way of putting it," I snarled, stopping and whirling to face her.

"Franny, come on." Tears pooled easily in her eyes. "What

did I do?" she repeated plaintively. She sounded pitiful. It was like yelling at a bunny rabbit.

"You could have been more discriminating about the company you kept. You were, like, hanging out with every loser in the school. Just totally embarrassing me."

The things that can come out of my mouth never fail to amaze me.

"Like who?" Zooey asked. "Like River?"

As angry as I was, I couldn't say anything mean about River. "I don't want to talk about this."

Zooey didn't give in. "Well, then I don't know who you mean. I thought you knew River from newspaper," she continued. "Was it other people? I was just having fun!"

"Forget it."

"I liked tonight. I *loved* it. I got to feel like someone else, someone with a real life. And I liked the people I met and they liked me and I'm sorry you didn't like me being there. I should have known better. I should never have trusted you to be mature enough not to flip out and get all jealous."

I shouldn't be trusted? "I was fine until . . ." I began, then trailed off.

"Until what?"

"Nothing," I muttered, turning around to open the door to our apartment. Inside, Dad was sitting on the couch, reading. At least he wasn't off with Celia.

"Hey, girls, how was the carnival?" he asked cluelessly.

"You know how that Malaysian mystic says the planet is going to be destroyed because this asteroid is going to smash into the earth and cause it go up in flames?"

Dad looked quizzically at me.

"It was so much worse than that could ever be."

The next morning, I left a hastily scribbled note for Dad on the kitchen counter, filled my backpack with everything I could possibly imagine needing, and headed out. When the going gets tough, it's best to evaporate.

I spent most of the day kicking around with Rhia. Zooey texted me a couple of times but, like the U.S. government, I had a policy against negotiating with terrorists. So I didn't reply.

Rhia suggested that I might be being a little unnecessarily harsh with Zooey, because Zooey had no idea that I liked River. She even said that being mad at Zooey was a cop-out because I was really mad at River for not paying more attention to me. I'm sure this was a reasonably astute explanation, but I sort of wished she'd just call him a jerk and be done with it.

When I was walking through the door that night, Carter called to see if I was still interested in going to *Frankenstein*. I felt a little bad agreeing, since I was obviously still hung up on River. But then I decided there was no point in not seizing the day. And anyway, I liked the Angelika.

"Mon dieu," Dad gasped in mock astonishment as I sailed into the living room an hour later. "Very nice." He nodded, examining my pleated mini, Stones T-shirt layered over a long-john top, Rhia's thoroughly fabulous black boots, and a newsboy hat I'd bought off the street that afternoon. My hair, which was almost permanently ponytailed, was loose for once and fashionably snarled to the best of my ability.

"Where are you off to?" he asked.

"Just a movie at the Angelika. *Frankenstein*. The old one, with Boris Karloff in it."

"Those boots are looking a little rock star for a movie."

I smiled what I hoped was a mysterious, alluring, uninformative smile. Franny Ford, Mona Lisa for the millennium. Dad wasn't fooled.

"There's a boy involved," he said confidently.

Another smile.

"Who is he? What's he like?"

"Male."

I wiggled my fingers in a quick wave and headed out before Dad could ask any more questions.

chapter 26

I loved the subway on Saturday nights. It felt like a city-wide party. Everybody was dressed up, and there was an air of excitement, and not quite as much shoving/spitting/cursing as usual. There have been times in my life when the subway has crawled so slowly that I thought I would be better off traveling by go-kart. Tonight, though, was not one of those nights, and when I got out at Bleecker Street, I found myself overwhelmed by the genuine intensity with which I heart NY.

Even though I was early, Carter had beaten me to the Angelika. When I saw him standing inside the lobby, a weird shiver ran through me.

"Hi," I said, wishing I could come up with a more exciting opener. But there was nothing wrong with "Hi." It was classic, really. And it never went out of style.

"Hi," Carter answered. "I got us tickets already. I ordered them online."

He did? That was really, really nice. And it involved planning and organization, something I was about as naturally skilled at as ice curling.

Shyly, we made our way into the theater and sat down. The Angelika was a very old, very cool, artsy theater. I hadn't realized people would be dressed up in Halloween costumes, and Carter and I spent a few minutes pointing out the best ones to each other.

As the lights were dimming and we were scooching down farther into our seats, I heard a very familiar laugh coming from the back of the auditorium, followed by a "dude" that had become almost equally familiar to me in the months since school had started. My head swiveled around. Hobbling toward me, like some actual horror movie creature spontaneously returned from the dead, was my sister. *And* she was actually wearing *my* favorite black shirt, as if she wasn't already the odds-on frontrunner for the Et Tu Brutus Traitor Award.

"Dude, we should've got here earlier," I heard River say. "There are no seats anywhere."

"That sounds like River." Carter sat up a little, looking around him.

I said nothing. I was back to silence being golden. Carter had unerringly picked one of the better first-date venues I could envision, but of course, so had River. Because River was River. I mean, he was *named* after a movie star who OD'd at the Viper Room. Of course he came to the Angelika. Annoyed, I watched as he and Zooey made their way down to the only two seats left in the house, which happened to be in the front row. The opening music was playing by now, and the rowdy crowd was either singing along or making "woooo-woooooo" fake scary sounds. I had a bird's-eye view of his head nestling into Zooey's.

I felt sick, and it had absolutely nothing to do with Frankenstein.

You cannot be a brat about this, I told myself as sternly as possible. What was the big shocker, really? I'd known Zooey had a date with River, because she'd told me. I just never thought that I would have to watch it unfold, scene by horrifying scene, in a way that made *Frankenstein* seem like *Sesame Street.*

Another scary thought sprang into my head.

If, for once, life worked out according to my fantasy and River somehow decided I *was* the girl for him, would that mean I crushed and humiliated Carter the way River had done to me?

Surreptitiously, I watched Carter out of the corner of my eye, singing happily along with the rest of the audience.

Jeez, he was cute.

He turned to look at me in sort of the same bemused way as Dr. Frankenstein was looking at the monster, so I joined half-heartedly in the merriment. And by the middle of the movie, I was feeling a lot better and had almost begun to believe that things would work out the way they were supposed to. I even snuggled down in my seat, just a small bit closer to Carter. There was a strange tingle coming off his body, like vapor off a cloud.

But then, as Boris Karloff contorted his sad, vacant face, my field of vision got invaded by River leaning over and turning Zooey's face toward him. I forgot about Carter and his vapor-tingle. I could see her skin, reflecting pale in the leftover light from the movie projection. Their lips brushed slightly, and then, again, more deeply. It was like this magnetic fabulous, freaking cinematic Scarlett-and-Rhett moment, except it was between River and Zooey.

Noooooo.

OK, maturity. I could totally be mature. Maybe I could go join a convent before there was any more damage to my already pancake-flat ego. It would be the sort of place where I would have to take a vow of silence and be contractually unable to talk to my sister for the rest of my life.

A large grunt from Frankenstein brought me back to the real world.

Weakly, I attempted to rejoin the fun with a feeble cheer. I could feel Carter shifting toward me, till our sleeves practically touched. I was conscious of the small space remaining between us, how slim it was, how easy it would be to shift positions—or, say, *breathe*—and then actually be touching each other. In front of me, River and Zooey were ravenously going after each other.

Watching them, I realized it had been a long time since I'd felt this upset about anything Zooey did.

It had been nice not to be jealous of her.

A small flutter at my elbow distracted me. I glanced down. Carter's sleeve now overlapped mine. I looked up, my eyes meeting his. He gave me a small, quick smile, then slid his hand to cover mine, the fingers wrapping over my own clenched ones. Without thinking, I let my hand unfurl.

Strangely, at that exact moment, I forgot that Zooey and River existed, forgot that their existence involved tongues, forgot that I was jealous, and that there were literally a hundred other rowdy people singing beside us.

Carter smiled again, his funny little flash of a smile. Without thinking, I leaned closer. ME. I was the one who moved first. And then, I felt his lips meet mine. Probably it was physics, bodies in motion staying in motion, and all that. But at that moment, it just felt very natural and very uncontrollable for us to keep going.

chapter 27

When we filed out of the theater an hour later, I felt like I had hit the jackpot on Emotional Turmoil. Three cheers for being so officially a teenager that the story of my life might as well be renamed *Angst and Angstier*. And, for once, my massive stash of books had failed, because I couldn't think of a single incident in which a heroine hopscotched from jealousy for one guy to kissing another in the awesome span of, um, five seconds.

"Would you mind waiting for me for a minute?" I asked Carter. "I just need . . ." what? A very strong cup of coffee? My head to stop whirling? "A pit stop," I finished.

"Sure." He shrugged agreeably. I made my way into the bathroom, where I leaned against the wall for a full five minutes, until my brain felt considerably less like a well-pureed liquid. Then I splashed a little water on my face, added a fresh layer of eyeliner, and headed back into the lobby. Carter had decided to occupy himself in my absence by talking to River and Zooey.

"Hi," I said quietly, sliding up next to him. He casually put his arm around my shoulder. It felt very heavy and very obvious.

"We thought we'd head over to Fanelli's, get something to eat," Carter said. "That sound OK?"

Or I could just throw myself onto the rack for a more direct form of anguish. I glanced at Zooey, who looked equally enthralled by the prospect.

"Sure," I agreed, allowing myself to be marched like a good little POW down to Prince Street. Fanelli's was packed, so we crowded around the only available table, which was meant for only two people. I could feel my knees bumping up against Carter's knees and against Zooey's cast.

"After that movie, I need food," River said, flipping his menu open. "A lot of it."

"Nothing like exhumed corpses to whet the appetite," Carter murmured, studying the menu himself. I giggled.

"Veggie burger and fries," River said to the waitress who had materialized beside him.

"Same, but a real burger," Carter said. "And extra ketchup."

"Just the fries," I said.

"And for you?" the waitress asked, looking at Zooey.

Zooey paused. I could almost hear the debate in her head about the salad she "should" get. "Same as her," she said firmly, nodding toward me. I thought about making a comment about how this was pretty much the first time Zooey had had fries since she was eight, but I didn't. I was working on what Mom referred to as "rising above." In another hour, I'd have risen so high that I could float through the Macy's Thanksgiving Parade.

"Are you a vegetarian?" Zooey asked River.

"Of course," River said casually. "I would never put a muscle in my mouth."

Ew.

Of course, if I were to have stopped and thought about it, I probably would have agreed that eating animals was not the most humane thing ever. The problem was that something like a hamburger bore such little resemblance to an actual animal that it never seemed like eating muscle to me. It was just *food.* Maybe that was why we—as in civilization, not as in people I knew personally—renamed foods. Like *beef* instead of *cow*, and *pork* instead of *pig*. It de-animaled it.

"Do you remember that time we went to Forest?" Zooey asked me as she salted her fries.

I rolled my eyes. "So our dad made us go to this restaurant where the whole big deal is that they own this game preserve and farm upstate and that's where all the food comes from."

"They had *pigeon* on the menu," Zooey said. River's cell phone, meanwhile, started beeping.

"The waiter kept talking about the official gamekeeper and how involved he was in getting the food," I added, watching River pull out his phone and start texting. "All I could think about was that the official gamekeeper was probably out in Union Square with a butterfly net."

Carter laughed. "I would rather eat toenails than eat pigeon."

"Wasting good food when there are starving Bohemians in this world. . . ." I said in fake dismay.

River let out a loud guffaw. "Sorry," he said, holding his phone up. "Funny text," he explained, his fingers moving rapidly across the keypad.

So it hadn't been me that had made him laugh.

"My friends are at the Adam Sandler fest right now," he added.

Adam Sandler? Not exactly my favorite.

"When there's *Frankenstein* in this world?" Carter asked.

"Dude, different strokes, you know?" he said, brushing the cinnamon-colored swag from his eyes.

"Sandler's like an unsung genius," he added.

Carter raised one eyebrow. "I'd actually say that, given his box office, he's oversung."

"I don't know that I've ever seen one of his movies," Zooey confessed.

"Really?" River asked. "Where have you been?" The way he said it wasn't very nice. An awkward lull settled over the tomorrow.

"In broken femur-ville," I threw in. "When you're dancing at Lincoln Center, it doesn't leave loads of time for fart-joke movies."

Everyone looked kind of surprised, but before someone could comment, River's phone beeped again. He crammed half his veggie burger into his mouth and reached for it. "Hang on, I wanna take this."

After he left, Carter looked at me. "Something wrong with fart jokes?"

"There's a ballerina at the table," I said. For some reason, I wasn't feeling that angry with Zooey anymore. "If you fill her ears with unpretty things, she loses her floatiness."

"Floatiness?" Carter said at the exact same time that Zooey said, "No!"

"Say whatever you want," she added. "I'm not that delicate."

River reappeared at her elbow. "You think we can get a beer here?" he asked, picking some fries off her plate.

Carter glanced around. "As in, they sell beer, yeah. Do I think you'd get carded? Probably."

"Whatever," River said. "I have a fake."

There was a pause while the waitress came over. "Can I get you anything else?" she chirped.

"What do you have on tap?" River asked.

The waitress looked at him but obligingly rattled off a few names.

River nodded. "OK, I'll have a glass of—"

"Milk?" The waitress asked sarcastically, cutting him off.

I laughed, despite myself. River glared at me. Zooey looked extremely uneasy.

"Nice try, peanut," the waitress said to River. "Anything else?"

"I have ID," River said.

"Sorry, not buying it," she said.

River looked irritated. "It's real."

The waitress smiled. "Yeah, and if your friend"—she pointed to me—"is over twelve, I'm a dancing rabbit."

Oh, no. *Me? I* was the reason she was turning down River?

"Sorry," I apologized as the waitress left, an automatic thick flush spreading over me.

"Why are you sorry?" Carter said. "You didn't do anything."

"Well, maybe if I weren't here, she wouldn't have been so suspicious."

"Forget it," River said. "It's not like there aren't other places to go." He sounded surly. "How 'bout we get out of here, babe?" he asked Zooey. "Go to a more kicking place?"

Zooey glanced at me and Carter. I couldn't figure out what the look meant. It should have been a *God, yes,* but something about it exuded ambivalence. "OK," she said. Then she grinned, a bit malevolently. "Let's blow this popsicle stand."

"Gee, Beav, your language," I said, just to annoy her.

She grinned and, strangely, I found myself grinning back.

chapter 28

Newspaper production should have been different after I kissed Carter. You would think it would be as obvious a change as getting lace henna-ed up your neck. But instead, here it was, four full days later, and the heavens hadn't opened, the world hadn't been enveloped into permanent sunset, and there were no violin sonatas accompanying my every step. Instead, production was just business as usual. River wore his fisherman's hat, Caroline was all perky, Carter himself was being hyperefficient, and I was so deeply lost in proofreading that aliens could have invaded and I wouldn't have noticed unless they were shaped like punctuation marks.

"There should be some layouts ready to go on the printer," Jonah said as I dropped my completed edits on his desk.

"Oh, and Franny, if you're going down the hall, will you stop by the vending machine?" Caroline broke in.

The printer is about fifteen feet down the hall. The vending machine is down the stairs, past the math and science wing, and through the cafeteria. It was like asking someone to stop off in Fargo on their way from New York to New Jersey.

"Sure," I answered, stretching my arms above my head. I needed a break, anyway.

"Hey, if you're going to the vending machine, would you run to Starbucks to get me a nonfat cappuccino with extra foam?" Brianna broke in, reaching for her purse.

"No problem." First-years, we live to serve.

Within a few minutes, I had a detailed shopping list and a

wad of money. By the time I made it to the printer, I was juggling a tray of drinks, bags of snacks, and some books Jonah had decided he wanted from his locker. I set everything down and grabbed the pages off the printer, scanning them to be sure they were the right ones. It was while I was looking them over that I heard voices moving toward me.

"Dude, what's your damage?" I heard River say very clearly.

"I just think maybe this is a real chance we could be missing."

That was Carter's voice. I turned around, trying to figure out where they were. Then I saw the edge of a uniform through the door. I was about to step into the hall to let them know I was there when River started talking again.

"Look, I know you've got the hots for her, but it's not going to happen."

I froze.

Me. They had to be talking about me. Unless Carter had the hots for someone else. Which would make this conversation the double-whammy of things I didn't want to hear.

"It's not about that," Carter insisted. "Yes, I like Franny, but I like her for the same reasons I think you should put her stuff in the paper. It's *smart*, River."

"She's a first-year."

"So?"

"So I'm not making a first-year our columnist." He sounded bored. How anyone could find this conversation boring was absolutely beyond me. I edged closer to the door.

"Why not?" Carter argued.

"Dude, don't you get it? *First-year*. End of story. I had to pay my dues, and so does she. That's the way the *Flyer* works. We don't give handouts."

"It's not a handout, River. We've been looking for a columnist forever. That State of Stanton article was *hilarious*. And she did a movie review that I can show you. People would read her. Just give her a try."

"Look, I get your point. I can see how she would be cool as a columnist. But not this year."

"You seriously think it's a better idea *not* to have a columnist than to give an opportunity to a first-year?" Carter sounded frustrated. "Am I missing something? If I could write the way Franny does, would you give me a columnist job? Just because I'm a second-year? Or why don't we just give it to Cassidy Petersen? I mean, she's been trashed since July and she only had the brainpower of gnat to begin with, but she *is* a fourth-year, so by your standards, she'd be the best option we have."

I smiled, despite myself.

"Knock it off, Carter. I'm not in the mood."

"You're being an *idiot*." Carter's voice had turned pleading. "I can't believe you're going to pass up this opportunity because you have some pointless idea about hierarchy. Besides, how could you not see how good this article is?"

"I am the editor in chief of this paper," River spat out. "And if you don't like the way I'm doing things, you can leave. We don't give gigs to first-years. That's Franny or anyone else. End of story."

I heard footsteps, then Carter swear quietly, then a few more footsteps. Stunned, I set the pages down on the printer and sank into a chair. I had made kind of a lot of excuses for River since I'd met him. Now, for the first time, I couldn't manage to give him the benefit of the doubt. If he had liquefied into an actual river and started flooding the school, I would have been less surprised. How could River—perfect, enlightened, *glorious* River—act like such a power-hungry jerk? I didn't know what to think.

And Carter? Um, *wow*. His armor was very, very shiny indeed.

I was pretty quiet the rest of production, just doing whatever needed to be done, trying to make sense of what I'd heard. For some reason, production moved super slowly, and by the time we got the paper to rest, it was way past the point when I was usually home.

"You ready to head?" Carter asked, coming over to where I was jamming my stuff back into my backpack.

"Yeah," I said awkwardly. I had had a million things to say to Carter on Saturday. Now I could barely manage monosyllables.

"Grab your coat; I'll walk you home," he said. He made it sound very natural.

It was late enough that the streets were reasonably quiet. As we walked uptown, I was silent, until I finally, *brilliantly*, managed, "Thanks for walking me home."

"Always a model of politeness, aren't you?" Carter said.

"Manners are a lost art," I answered automatically. Then, because I couldn't stand it any longer, I added, "OK, I think I overheard something I wasn't supposed to earlier."

"Yeah?" Carter asked, very blasé. I might as well have been talking about the weather.

"I heard you talking to River. I don't think you knew I was there and—" I paused. "And I probably should have said I could hear you, except I didn't really know how to interrupt."

"Oops," Carter said. Then he added, "That must have been weird."

"Well, you know," I said, using my words, so powerfully, once again.

"I mean . . ." Carter paused, sounding pretty inarticulate himself. "Especially since I know how much you like River."

I stopped. In my tracks, frozen, as completely inanimate as rock, paper, *and* scissors. How could Carter have known that?

Or did he mean "like," as in merely "enjoy"? As in *I like the color blue.*

"Sure, I like River," I fudged casually. "I mean, he makes newspaper a lot of fun."

"Sometimes it seems like you like *like* him."

Um.

"How did you know that?"

Carter smiled. "It's been kind of obvious, Franny."

"Oh," I repeated, solidifying my long-standing title as Queen of the Monosyllables. We kept walking in silence. It felt OK, though, the same sort of comfortable quiet as I used to have hanging out with Dad. When we hit a small park, I gestured to the benches. It probably wasn't the greatest idea to sit in the square at this time of night, but I wanted to hang out for a bit. Besides, there *were* plenty of people going in and out of the subway nearby.

"You're right," I said after what seemed like a very long while. "I do like River. Like, *like* River," I emphasized. "Or at least I have like *liked* him." I sounded like a Valley Girl convention. "But it's pretty confusing, because I have also started to like someone else." Then, just to be clear, I added, "Like like."

"Like who?" Carter asked, playing along.

I turned to face him, enjoying the familiarity of his by-now-very-familiar face. "Like you," I said simply. "I like you."

And, at that moment, I realized that it was all true! All the books I'd read and movies I'd seen . . . when you said something special to someone special, the world really did stop moving, and there was this awesome silence. All I wanted to do was bask in it, forever.

But, because this was New York, it was a far briefer moment than it might have been elsewhere. After only a mere second of our gazing into each other's eyes, a homeless man lurched over.

"C'mon, help a guy, cold tonight," he muttered, a disintegrating cigarette stuck in one corner of his mouth.

I heart NY. But not at this moment. I dug in my pocket and found some spare change and the guy wandered off.

"Did you mean what you said about my writing?" I asked.

Carter made a little wry facial expression in response. I loved how expressive he could be without ever saying anything.

"Point taken. Well, thanks for believing in me," I conceded. "But, I guess I'm not going to be a columnist until I lick some more boots."

"Which is *idiotic*," Carter said.

I shrugged. "It's the way it is."

"It's not OK."

We were quiet for a while. "Now can I ask you something?" I said at last.

"Sure."

"Why did you even ask me out if you thought I liked River?"

"I just wanted to." He shrugged. "I guess I'm cocky enough. Or else I just liked you enough."

I leaned into him. "I'm glad you did. Really glad." I took his hand in mine and held it. "I think maybe there was a part of me that *thought* River and I would be so amazing together, but maybe I didn't know him very well."

As the words came out, I realized they were true.

"I've been pretty nasty to Zooey since she went out with him," I added. "I just get tired of always being second fiddle to her, you know?"

Carter leaned back and put his arm around me. "Second fiddle? To Zooey?"

"I dunno; I guess it's sour grapes, or maybe normal sibling rivalry. It's stupid, really. I just sometimes think she lucked out. Like she'll be famous because of her ballet. She pretty much *is* famous because of it already. And she's prettier and everyone always likes her and . . ." I trailed off.

"Wow," Carter said. "Do you really think that?"

Did I?

"I used to. I'm less sure now. But, yeah, generally."

"My brother got in a big fight with my parents over the summer," Carter said. "He didn't want to go back to college and they obviously wanted him to, and then they went through his stuff and found some pot and freaked out. And he just left. Went to Paris, actually, and we haven't heard anything since. Not a phone call or an e-mail or anything. I doubt he'll be back for Thanksgiving."

"I'm sorry," I said.

"I guess all I'm saying is that things change in families and you sometimes don't know how they're going to change."

"Yeah," I agreed.

Carter wrapped his arms around me. I wouldn't have been surprised if he had kissed me, but this big cuddly bear hug was completely unexpected and so tender I was afraid it might make me cry. I also knew that he wasn't so much comforting me as needing a hug himself right now. Reflexively, I curled my head into his shoulder. The wool of his coat prickled uncomfortably, but I didn't want to move. He smelled like sandalwood soap, a good clean *male* smell.

"You know," Carter said after a while, "I don't know where you got the idea that Zooey is prettier than you."

"Uh, my retina?"

"I like the way *you* look," he said. "A lot. She's obvious in every way. You"—he stroked my hair—"are a surprise."

chapter 29

If you could have dinner with any three people, living or dead, who would they be and why?

I hated that question. I thought it was completely predictable. The answers almost always involved some variation of Jesus, Gandhi, George Washington, and Mother Theresa. Since I'd never actually bothered to make my own list, I couldn't say for sure who would make the cut. But I had a sneaking suspicion that Mother Teresa and George Washington would be out in the cold. Leprosy was contagious, and Washington didn't have any teeth anyway.

One thing I *didn't* get was why people weren't practical with these lists. Seriously, if you're having a dinner party, you ought to go for one of the Iron Chefs, Julia Child, or Martha Stewart. Because cooking was not the easiest thing on the planet, and while I generally adored takeout, it got old after a while. I was at the stage where a perfectly respectable tuna and avocado roll was turning me green.

All of which was why I had pulled our cookbooks down from the shelf over the toaster and was flipping through the pages. But I also had a more important ulterior motive than food. I wanted to see if I could lure Dad home at a reasonable time. And, after an hour passed without his responding to my first text, it was time for more direct action.

"Dexter Boutique, this is Celia."

Hmmph.

"It's Franny. Is my dad there?"

"Um, certainly." Celia sounded less polished than usual. "He's right here." I tried not to wonder what she meant by "right" here.

"Franny?"

"Hi, Daddy, I'm going to cook something for dinner. Will you come home?"

"Cook?" he asked.

"I even bought vegetables."

"Well, I do have a lot of stuff to get done here," he began.

I held my breath.

"But, OK. Someone has to make sure you don't burn the house down, I suppose."

Burn down the house? Please. I had a recipe. How hard could it be?

An hour later, Dad still wasn't home, and I was rethinking my brilliant idea. I had never cooked anything more complicated than brownie mix before, and our kitchen was a total disaster. And it turned out that recipes, like boys, needed to master the art of saying exactly what they meant.

"This place looks like Disaster Central," Zooey said, thumping into the kitchen.

"I'm cooking," I said through gritted teeth as I stirred soup.

"You're cooking?" Zooey sounded puzzled.

"Yes." A stray pink peppercorn flew out of the pot and hit me on the cheek. With my luck, it would scar. And not a delicate, refined beauty mark kind of scar, but the kind of scar that looked like a permanent zit.

Zooey looked over my shoulder at the cookbook. "Oooh, are you making this squash thingy?"

In my book, squash ranked right up there with rodents and uranium in the category of Things You Should Never Put in Your Mouth. "No, soup." I pointed to the recipe. As I did, my sleeve dragged across the counter, knocking over a bottle of olive oil. It shattered, with a big splash of oil drenching my legs. I watched as the vast golden puddle spread across the floor.

"Is that burning?" Zooey pointed to my pot. "Something smells like it's burning. Is it supposed to smell like that?" She delicately stepped over the broken glass and sat down at the kitchen table.

"Um, do you think you can help me?" I asked Zooey, who had started texting on her cell phone.

"In a second," she answered. "I just want to send this."

And Nero fiddled while Rome burned. . . .

Grumpily, I stared at the onions smoking in the bottom of the pot. It had taken a half hour to chop all the onions, and now they were welded to the pot.

"I can't believe this. I followed the directions exactly," I said, trying to chisel the charcoal onion pieces from the bottom of the pot with a spatula. As I did, my elbow somehow brushed against the burner. I could hear a hiss as the skin on my arm seared.

"Ahhhhh!"

Zooey looked up casually from her cell phone. "What happened?"

"Burn," I gasped. "My arm."

Nero made sympathetic "The Coliseum was a really pretty building" sounds.

I staggered over to the freezer and began dumping ice into a dish towel. "I'm so annoyed," I wailed, holding the towel to my arm and simultaneously attempting to wipe oil off my feet.

"Why were you trying to cook anyway?" she asked.

"Clearly, I got brainwashed by aliens." Probably that eerie white light shining outside our kitchen window wasn't from the earth-saving twisty bulb in the laundry room of the Finkels' apartment. It was probably the mother ship waiting to beam me up.

"I had this stupid idea that maybe Dad would come home for dinner," I admitted. "But he said he would be here and he isn't yet and when I called the store, Celia answered."

Zooey frowned. "I went over there the other day."

"To the store?"

"Mmm-hmm. I met Celia."

"And?"

"Well, Dad wasn't around. But she kind of made Heidi Klum look a sack of Doritos."

I giggled.

"Hey, I have to ask something," Zooey said. "Are you still mad at me?"

I pondered, briefly. Did I need to confess my massive crush on River? Or apologize for stomping around like Attila the Hun?

"I don't think so," I said, surprising myself by how much I didn't want to be mad at Zooey.

"Good." Zooey texted something on her phone, then set it down. "Anyway, if it was about River, you should know that I don't really like him."

I hadn't seen that coming.

Zooey heaved herself upward and lurched toward the sink, leaning heavily on her crutch as she filled a glass of water. "Our date was *awful*," she continued, taking a long swallow.

"Really?"

"I mean, the best part was when we were hanging out with you and Carter. After that, we went to some awful party where he either talked about himself or name-dropped about me the whole night." She rolled her eyes and put on a deep voice, much deeper than River's actual voice. "Dude, you've seen Zooey on the subway posters; she was gonna be Juliet till she crashed." She rolled her eyes again. "He's so into me now, Franny. I can't get him to stop calling. But he doesn't like me."

"But if he's calling all the time?" I questioned.

"No." Zooey shook her head. "He likes the idea of dating some hot ballerina. He doesn't like *me*. Half the time, when I'm talking, I feel like I'm boring him." She shrugged. "And when he talks, it's never really *to* me; it's *at* me, like I'm supposed to sit there and be *sooo* impressed that he's the editor of the paper and all newshoundy."

I felt myself start to flush, thinking of how bowled over I'd been by River. There was a time when knowing River was single would have catapulted me into glee. Now, I felt nothing—other than surprise that I felt nothing.

chapter 30

Once upon a time, some genius scientist decided that the best place to study chaos theory was in outer space. They could have just come to the Stanton cafeteria at lunch. It had taken me two and half months to figure out where first-years could sit without getting pelted with French fries by upperclassmen and which of the six different lunch lines would let me get my food in less than half an hour. But one of the things I actually *liked* about the cafeteria was that it gave me a few minutes during the day just to hang out with people and do something that had nothing to do with geometry or English. A few days after the cooking disaster, Rhia and I were happily absorbed in reading our horoscopes when someone lifted the magazine from my hand. I looked up.

"Hi!" Zooey chirped, sounding as natural as if we'd run into each other in our living room.

"Hi," I replied automatically. Then, "What are you doing here?"

She settled herself into the chair next to me. "Well, I guess you could say I followed you to school."

"Like Mary's little lamb?" Rhia asked.

Zooey giggled. "Well, I was so bored at home just doing independent study over and over, and I thought I'd come and have lunch with you." She swung a plastic bag onto the table. "I even brought a picnic."

Rhia shrugged at me. Surprised, I shrugged slightly in return, watching Zooey unpack grapes, a wedge of cheese, a loaf of bread, a bottle of iced green tea, and keep going. It was sort of like Mary Poppins's carpet bag; I kept wondering what would come out next.

"Thanks," I said. Technically, we weren't allowed school visitors, and Zooey, in her jean jacket and miniskirt, was not exactly what I would call inconspicuous. But it's not like anyone but students was around anyway. "We're checking out our horoscopes," I said, pushing the magazine over to her.

"Hmm," she said, taking the magazine from me. "I better be going on a long journey someplace."

"It's a horoscope, not a fortune," I started, but before I could finish, Curt Marino swung in beside us.

"Hey," he said happily, touching Zooey's shoulder. "Franny didn't tell me you were coming."

"Hi," Zooey said.

"You need anything? Can I get you something? What about a smoothie?"

"I'm fine, really," she said. "I brought lunch."

"This is so awesome you're here." Curt was talking kind of loudly, and I realized people were starting to notice us.

"Is that your sister?" Jenny Wong leaned over from the table behind me. "I heard about her."

I wondered exactly what she had heard. In addition to chaos theory, the cafeteria was also the best possible place to start a rumor.

"Zooey, we're not really supposed to have guests at school," I said. "I mean, it's great that you came, but I'm wondering if maybe you should not be here?"

"I'm not a *guest*," Zooey said. "I'm your sister. Relatives are different."

"I'm not sure they are," I said.

"What's the big deal, Franny?" Elton Garland said, materializing from behind me. "I mean, it's not like Zooey's some criminal."

"I dunno," I said, watching more people gather. "Let me walk you out."

"Franny!" Zooey said.

"Look, maybe I'm being silly, but you're really not supposed to be here—and I have class in like ten minutes anyway."

Elton slung an arm around Zooey's shoulder. "So go to class. We'll take care of your sister."

"Dude, don't touch her," Curt said.

"You don't talk to her," Elton shot back.

This was getting a little insane. "Zooey," I pleaded, watching more people flock over.

"I'll see you at home, Franny," she said confidently. "Really. I'll just hang out here for a few minutes, then I'll head."

I looked at her dubiously for a moment. Then, grabbing my lunch tray, I turned away from the table. Rhia picked up her lunch box. "I'll go with you," she said quietly.

I didn't realize Curt had followed us out until we were almost to the door. Glancing warily at Rhia, he whispered he had something private to tell me.

"What?" I hadn't talked to Curt (or, really, even seen him) since the Halloween carnival.

"You have to help me. I am obsessed with your sister." His face was flushed. "I've never seen anyone like her."

I really wanted his mouth to stop moving.

"I've been writing a poem for her." He looked down at the table. "Blank verse, of course. I couldn't figure out what rhymed with Zooey."

Toe-y. "That's nice," I offered.

"Franny," Curt repeated, looking vaguely anguished. His preppy, generally combed hair was hanging in his face, and there was a button missing on his uniform. "Your sister, Franny. She's unbelievable. River beat me at the carnival, but he's not going to beat me again.

"When I saw her today, I knew I needed to tell her about the poem. I need to make a grand gesture." He actually brought his hand to his chest and clasped his heart as he talked. In about three more seconds, he would have on white gloves and a feather in his hat.

I didn't know what to say. "I should get going," I managed. Then, "Good luck!"

Half an hour later, I was deep into (another) quiz in English, when there was a knock on the classroom door. Somehow, I wasn't surprised when Ms. Hurley read the note handed to her and stopped beside my desk.

"There's a message for you," she said quietly.

I followed her into the hallway.

"Franny, I'm afraid you're wanted in the principal's office."

In my entire life, I had never had a message like this. I contemplated banging my head against the wall hard enough to require immediate medical attention, but not hard enough to do any lasting damage. Instead, coward that I am, I just slunk as slowly as I possibly could through the halls.

"Hi," I said to the receptionist, once I finally meandered in. "I'm Franny Ford. I got a message to come here."

She looked up from her computer and smiled sympathetically at me.

"I think they've been waiting for you."

"Is it, uh, my sister?" I asked, even though I pretty much knew the answer.

"You can go ahead and go in," the receptionist said diplomatically.

Sighing, I opened the door. I had assumed it was just going to be Zooey inside. Instead, I was greeted by the rather stunning sight of Zooey, Curt, Elton, and two kids I had never seen before. Smoothie dripped from their hair, and their uniforms were splashed with tomato sauce and salad dressing. A clump of pizza cheese clung to Curt's neck. There was spinach in Zooey's ear.

My perfect ballerina sister. In a *food fight.* Food she would never even eat was falling out of her hair.

"Ah, the other Ms. Ford," Principal Harrow began. "Why don't you have a seat?" His white shirt looked even snowier and more immaculate in contrast to everyone else's sliminess.

Well, he wouldn't expel me just because of Zooey. He couldn't.

"As you know, your sister, who is not a member of our community, violated school security today. She impersonated a Stanton student in order to gain access to the cafeteria. This might have gone unnoticed, were it not for the small fact that she instigated more havoc than we have ever seen in the history of the school."

"I didn't impersonate anyone," Zooey broke in. "I just didn't answer that guy when he asked if I went to school here."

"Ms. Ford," Principal Harrow began. "We have been through this." He looked at me. "From what I understand, you were aware of this breach."

Um, breach? It was a cafeteria, not an airport.

"I knew she was in the cafeteria," I admitted.

"Franny tried to get me to leave. It's not her fault." Zooey sighed loudly. "I told you that."

Principal Harrow leaned closer to me. "And you chose not to tell anyone, which would have been an error of judgment on your part."

Well, yeah, but I made errors of judgment every other second. Not that I needed to share that charming tidbit aloud.

"Nevertheless, you are not held responsible for your sister or your classmates."

Curt Marino hung his head. Elton stared surlily ahead. One of the other boys, whom I'd never seen before, actually winked at me. Surprised, I winked back.

"I told you," Zooey said again. "Franny wasn't even there when the food fight happened."

"And," Principal Harrow said to me, "I can appreciate the difficulty of communicating with your sister at times, given her . . ." He paused, trying to think of the most polite way phrase it. "Stubbornness," he settled. He looked at me with an expression that was almost—but not quite—kind. I found myself smiling weakly at him.

"Obviously, there will be consequences for all of the individuals directly involved. As your sister is not a Stanton student, we thought it made sense for you to be present when we contacted your father."

Zooey slouched in her chair. "I didn't throw anything," she muttered. Some people make waves; I had to have the sister who made tsunamis.

"Can I just go back to class?" I asked. "Because this isn't really about me."

"I think you better stay."

Bleh.

chapter 31

When Dad finally retrieved Zooey and me from school, there were more fireworks than on the Fourth of July, Bastille Day, and New Year's Eve combined. Think explosions all the way through the cab ride home, in the lobby, up the elevator, culminating in a massive grand finale in our living room.

"It's what I told you already." Zooey stormed as she threw open the apartment door. "I just wanted to see what lunch in a real high school was like. I didn't know there would be smoothie tossing involved." She dropped her coat onto the floor. "And besides, I told you already. I personally did not throw any food."

"But you were the entire reason they were throwing stuff," Dad countered.

"That's not my fault. I didn't tell them to chuck smoothies at each other. They should know better. I can't control the imbeciles of this world."

"So I'm going to go to my room," I called to them, heading toward the hallway.

"No," Dad and Zooey answered at exactly the same time. I groaned. Why couldn't they fight amongst themselves?

"Franny, tell Dad how *crazy* Curt was being. Like there was no way I could have stopped him from starting that fight. Unless I had a straitjacket."

"I get it," Dad snapped. "I heard you the first ten times." He heaved himself into the couch and put his forehead on his hands. Zooey looked at me. I shrugged.

"Daddy?" she said.

He was quiet. Zooey went and sat down on the couch next to him.

"I'm sorry," she said.

Silence.

"And, Franny, I guess I should have listened to you when you said I should go." She wrinkled her nose. "I never thought things would go so wrong. Or that you would get dragged into it."

"S'OK," I muttered. I wasn't exactly filled with the spirit of forgiveness, but an apology was an apology.

Dad took his head out of his hands. "I suppose what I don't get is what's been going on with the two of you lately. You *never* used to act this way. Charging clothes on my credit card, food fights. . . ." He looked directly at me. "Slipping grades?

"I know it's been a big adjustment for us to have Mom gone," he added.

That was sort of like saying the *universe* had had a big adjustment when the Big Bang happened.

"But you can't continue like this." He shook his head. "You have to change the way you're acting."

"We," I corrected him, before I realized it.

"What?"

"Don't you mean *we*? That *we* have to change what we're doing?" The big lump in my throat made it hard to talk. "Because it's not just me and Zooey screwing up, you know," I continued.

There was a fairly awesome silence. Not awesome like, "Groovy, dude," but the real definition of awesome: impressive and terrifying all at once. I felt a small bubble of anger in my gut and bit my lip to keep from losing it.

"I know I haven't been around as much as I could," Dad said at last.

Still biting my lip, I looked at Zooey. Her jaw was clenched so tightly that she almost looked ugly.

"It's not just that," she started. "I mean, yeah. You're never here. You make us take care of *everything* on our own. I can barely walk and Franny's the one who's been there for me."

I hadn't thought of what I was doing as "being there" for Zooey. It sounded very grown-up.

"But we know about Celia," she said.

The words clattered into the air.

"How could you do something like that?" she added. "Don't you care about us?" Tears started slipping down her face. "Everything falls apart and you do something that makes it so much worse. How could you?"

"Celia?" he asked. He sounded calm, like we were talking about weather, or what we should have for dinner.

"Don't lie," Zooey said.

"I'm just a little confused," he answered.

"We know you're having an affair with Celia," Zooey answered flatly.

I was so, so glad Zooey had been the one to say it aloud. I was crying as well; the whole collar of my shirt was slimy with tears. I wished I could close my eyes, click my heels, and land somewhere—anywhere—else, even if it wasn't technically on the other side of the rainbow.

"Franny," Dad said. He patted the couch on the other side of him. "Come here."

"No."

"Please."

"Is it true?" I asked. Up until now, the Celia issue had felt fake, something that really couldn't happen to me and my family. But suddenly, it felt as real as the slimy tears on my face or the small blister on my heel.

"Is it *true*?" I repeated, loudly.

"No," Dad said at last. He patted the space next to him again. "It's not true." A small, rueful smile appeared on his face.

"I swear I am not having an affair with Celia. I actually don't know where you girls got that idea. She's extremely good at her job but has always seemed a little like a cyborg to me."

I moved onto the couch beside him and he put his arms around me.

"It's because you've been spending every night working late," I said. "And you never used to and she's always there and she's all bootsy and glammy and she always acts like we're interrupting and WHY ELSE WOULD YOU BE THERE ALL THE TIME?"

"We haven't seen you in weeks," Zooey added. "We wouldn't even have found the time to have this conversation if I hadn't gotten into a food fight." She looked pointedly at him.

Dad stretched his other arm around her.

"I'm so sorry," he said. He sounded small, not like my dad at all. "You guys are . . ." He paused. "Completely right. Not about Celia, though.

"Celia's Celia. I hired her for the same reasons that I haven't been home much, but it has nothing to do with me liking her. Having your mom gone has been so much harder than I ever thought it would be. It's hard for me to be in our apartment without her. And it's hard for me to get stuff done at work.

"Celia, for the record, is probably not going to be around much longer. She hasn't said anything. But I have a feeling that working in a store isn't where she wants to be."

He sighed. "I'm sorry about everything."

I leaned against him. "Me too."

chapter 32

The next day, I tried to convince Dad that I should stay home from school, just to recuperate and give the family time to reconnect with one another. Obviously, we couldn't expect one tearjerky conversation to turn us into the Brady Bunch. And if I didn't go to school, there would be plenty of time for us to bond and read self-help books in between the movie marathon and late afternoon pedicures.

When he is eighty, my dad is not going to be one of those people who gets swindled out of his life savings by a slick-talking con artist. He is going to be the person who locks the con artist in the broom closet while he calls the FBI and plasters the guy's picture all over the Internet. I'll be the one hovering outside the closet door saying things like, "Make sure he has enough oxygen!"

Needless to say, I made it to Stanton just as the first bell was ringing. I noticed a few stares as I slid into my chair in homeroom. Not that I blamed people for ogling. Food fights were the sort of thing that happened in *Animal House*, not in our ho-hum little neck of the woods. Still, by the time lunch rolled around, I was sick of all the buzzes and whispers and glances that seemed to trail me wherever I went.

"Shall we revisit the scene of the crime?" Rhia asked sympathetically as I paused at the cafeteria entrance.

"It's either that or starve," I agreed.

Principal Harrow had squawked a lot yesterday about the cleaning costs from the food fight (which Dad and the other parents were going to have to cover). Evidently the bleach bills had been put to good use, because the cafeteria looked exactly the same as it always had.

It was when I was on my way to the stir fry station that a funny thing happened. A guy I had never seen before wandered up to me. "Are you Franny?" he asked.

"Yeah," I answered, bracing myself for some comment on Zooey's remarkable hotness.

"You're my hero," he said bluntly.

Excuse me?

"Sarcasm will get you nowhere," I answered.

"No, seriously. You're like a rock star." He flipped a piece of new gum onto my tray and sauntered off.

Weird. Weird. Weird.

"I feel like things are weird today," I said as I sat down across from Rhia at our regular table. "Like people are staring at me and this guy just came up to me and said I was his hero and . . ." I trailed off. "It's just all very strange."

"It's probably just the Zooey aftermath," Rhia said, taking a sip of water.

I was about to agree when Jenny Wong, who was sitting a few seats over, sidled down next to me.

"It's not about your sister," she said confidingly. "It's you."

ME?

"You know, it's all that stuff you said. *Everyone* is talking about it. I've never seen anything like it."

What could I have said? I was the world's most easily intimidated human. If someone looked at me the wrong way, I saw my shadow and ran into a hole. I rethought the conversations with Zooey and in Principal Harrow's office. Nothing seemed particularly gossip-worthy.

"My favorite part was when you talked about the new library

chairs. You know, that they smelled like jelly shoes." Jenny giggled.

Jellies? I was pretty sure I had said nothing to Principal Harrow about jellies.

"And that stuff about the new uniforms was hilarious."

OH MY GOD. Those were things I'd said in my State of Stanton article, the one River had axed. How could people have read it?

Baffled, I stared at my palm, like maybe it could give me a clue.

"What are you doing?" Jenny asked.

"Reading my own palm." Duh.

Jenny howled. "You're awesome, girl."

Maybe I had fallen through a rabbit hole, into some surreal new world, where people loved everything I said and did. "Jenny, listen. You *have* to tell me where you saw all this stuff. Was it in the paper?"

"Yeah, of course," she said.

The only article I should have had in the paper this week was the Campus Crime Summary, involving two stolen iPods and one illegally pulled fire alarm. This was not good. "I need to find a copy."

"Do I still have it? " Jenny started rummaging through her bag, tossing out notebooks and a hat. She was probably moving at a normal pace, but it seemed like slow motion.

"I have to see the paper," I repeated, looking wildly around the cafeteria. "I need to figure out what's going on."

"Yeah, you do need to figure that out," an angry voice said behind me. I turned. It was Brianna Bronstein. "And, by the way, that goes for your sister too."

River, beside her, had just as ugly an expression on his face. Apparently, this was not some enchanted rabbit hole world where I had a starring role as America's Most Beloved.

"Give Zooey a break," I answered. "It's not her fault River and all those other guys like her."

"Forget your sister," River said, stepping closer. "This is about what you did, Franny."

WHAT I DID? Did I have amnesia?

"I'm having trouble figuring out quite what's going on right now," I began. *How* had the article gotten in the paper?

"You bet you are," River said. "You are off the *Flyer.* Just get that clear. I don't want to see you at meetings, at production, in the offices. I don't even want to see the paper in your hand."

My stomach suddenly felt very acrobatic.

"As of today, you are dead to us," he said.

"But people liked my article," I said, feeling very scared but also kind of awed by what was happening. Total strangers had agreed with something that I really believed in.

"You little brat," Brianna started again.

"I can't believe you need an explanation," River said. "I was so right not to have listened to Carter about you."

"River," I said faintly, not sure whether to be scared or terrified or what.

"Lay off Franny," Jenny broke in. "You guys are just jealous of her."

"Whatever," Brianna said.

"You are," Jenny insisted. "It's so obvious."

She had finally found her copy of the *Flyer*, and she slapped it on the table. There it was: my State of Stanton article, front and center, with a headline roughly the size of Montana. Next to the byline was a small photo of me, just in case there was any confusion.

"That article was unauthorized," River said, the clove-colored eyes flat and cold.

It seemed impossible that I had ever liked him. "So is every single Madonna biography," I shot back.

"I can't believe you snuck that in the paper," River said. "You know what I thought about it. I told you."

"I didn't do it," I emphasized. "Look, I get why you're pissed, but I seriously don't know how this happened."

"Lucky for you, it did," River sneered. "You just couldn't do things the way they're meant to be done."

"River, I did NOT put this article in the paper."

"Then who did?" Brianna asked.

"Well, Carter took the layouts to the printer," River started, then stopped, as the same thought occurred to all of us.

Apparently, Curt Marino wasn't the only one who felt like making a grand gesture for a Ford sister.

chapter 33

Just like yesterday, the note came in the middle of English. Ms. Hurley stopped talking about sonnets to read it.

"Franny?" she said disapprovingly. "Can you come into the hall for a second?"

A massive buzz filled the room. You could have powered all of Norman, Oklahoma, with the energy.

"People!" She clapped her hands pointlessly. "Quiet, please." The room continued to vibrate. Gloomily, I followed her out into the hallway, where she crossed her arms and looked at me expectantly.

"I know," I said, wincing. "I'm probably wanted in the principal's office."

"Are you having any sense of déjà vu, Franny? Or is that just me?"

"I know it seems bad. But it's just a series of unfortunate events." I looked at her dubious face. "I can see you don't believe me."

"I thought when I saw your article in the paper that maybe things were going a little easier for you." She shook her head. "I have to tell you that was a great bit of writing."

"Thanks." I gestured to the note. "But not everyone was so thrilled with the article."

Ms. Hurley's eyebrows went up. "Is that why Principal Harrow wants to see you?" she said. "Because of what you wrote?"

"I don't think it's as much *what* I wrote but that it wasn't supposed to be in the paper at all. The editor cut it."

"Cut the article? Because it was controversial?"

I shook my head, and briefly explained the situation. As I talked, she looked increasingly annoyed.

"It's not that big a deal," I said, watching her brows draw together.

"Franny, it is."

"The article made it in the paper," I said. "People got to read it and all the time I spent working on it didn't go to waste."

"This isn't the way it should have happened." Ms. Hurley sighed. "I had no idea this sort of thing was going on with the newspaper." She shook her head. "It's unacceptable."

Something about her anger touched me. "Thanks," I offered.

"Franny," she started. "Don't be nice about this article. When you get to Mr. Harrow's office, stick up for yourself more than you're doing right now."

"OK," I said, surprised.

She gave me a sort of weary look. "You never read *Franny and Zooey*, did you?" I shook my head. "You should, simply because you'll like it," she said. "But in terms of your English grade, I'm thinking your article is plenty good enough to count for extra credit. Any piece of writing that good deserves bonus points." I opened my mouth to thank her, but she pointed toward the office. "Good luck."

I started down the hall with trudging steps. Despite everything, I had a feeling I was going to need an entire four-leaf clover field worth of luck.

When I got to the office, Carter was slouched on the bench outside, staring at the floor and picking his cuticles.

"What's a nice guy like you doing in a place like this?" I asked, sinking onto the bench beside him. He didn't answer. "Hey," I tried again.

"I think I screwed up, Franny. Screwed up very, very bad," he emphasized, turning to look at me. "Seriously, I am so sorry I put you in this position."

"I was going to say thank you," I said quietly. "Everyone is talking about something I wrote. That's unbelievably cool."

"I don't know what I was thinking," Carter continued, as if I hadn't said anything. "I spent all morning telling everyone I saw to read the article. I couldn't possibly have been *more* obvious."

"I think it's awesome," I said. Overwhelming, to be sure, but definitely awesome. It made me feel, well, not exactly important, but more like what I cared about was important. This may sound dippy, but I hadn't known I had strong feelings about anything worthwhile until now.

The phone at the receptionist's desk rang. She looked over at us. "You can go in."

Thankfully, it was just River inside the principal's office, and not Brianna also. His face was surprisingly red and flushed. I stared. It was undeniable: River McGee was blushing. Karma could be so delicious.

"I was delighted this morning," Principal Harrow began, "to see that our school paper had mustered some new talent."

Despite the awkward heaviness hanging over us like a mushroom cloud, I felt myself warm. *Talent* and *delight* weren't words I typically associated with myself.

"Yet, it appears the way this article got into the paper was not so delightful."

Carter continued to stare at the floor in a defeated manner. My heartstrings twanged just watching him. Knights in shining armor should never look so anguished.

"While Mr. McGee and I have exchanged some words about what constitutes being an editor versus a dictator, I think we can all agree that the ultimate manner in which this situation was handled was grossly unorthodox."

Carter still hadn't looked up. The twanging heartstrings were now going overtime. In another moment, they would probably break out in "The Devil Went Down to Georgia."

I couldn't take it. It was just going to have to be a day for grand gestures.

"I know, Principal Harrow," I said as calmly as I could. "I'm sorry. I was so angry at River that I put the article in yesterday when I took the layout to the printer. It's all my fault. No one else was involved."

There was minor pandemonium in the room. Forget worms. I had somehow opened a can of vipers.

"Franny, no!" Carter said.

"She's lying," River cut in. "She didn't know a thing about it an hour ago."

"I lied to you earlier," I said to River. "Carter asked me to take the layout in and I made the switch then."

"Franny," Carter broke in.

Principal Harrow leaned across the desk. "You seem to have found your voice since yesterday, Ms. Ford," he said to me.

"Franny didn't do it," Carter said again, "I did. Because I *hated* that River was so hung up on himself that he couldn't see how good she was."

Principal Harrow started to say something, but the door to the office flew open before he could get the words out.

Zooey.

The disaster otherwise known as my life ratcheted up another point on the Richter scale.

"What are you saying to my sister?" she yelled. "Lay off of her."

Principal Harrow's eyes widened to roughly the circumference of Jupiter. I cringed in anticipation.

"Ms. Ford," he said sharply. "I thought we established that you did not belong on the Stanton premises yesterday." His voice could have started a second Ice Age. Probably, somewhere in the Yukon, glaciers were already starting to creep downward.

"I know. And I thought about it and I decided I felt really bad, so I came back to apologize. But now I realize how CRAZY that was." She looked at me. "Come on, Franny, let's go. I don't want them to keep kicking you around for something I did."

"Oh, Zooey," I began.

"We are not talking about yesterday's shenanigans," Principal Harrow fumed. "It seems the Ford sisters are alike in their tendency to wreak havoc in this school."

"Zooey, there's a little situation going on," I said. "You really should leave. It's not the food fight."

"Like I would leave you alone in Fascist Central." She sat down next to me and propped her crutches against my chair. "Trust me, Franny. I was in here yesterday and you would not believe some of the things that went down." She sniffed. "We would never put up with that treatment at the ballet academy. Now," she said, staring directly at Principal Harrow. "I think you better tell me what's going on."

My jaw dropped.

"Because, Principal Harrow." She said his name like it tasted bad. "I know my sister and I know she doesn't need to be in here."

"I agree," said a voice from the doorway. We turned to see Ms. Hurley standing there. The Richter scale accumulated another point.

"I'm sorry, Principal." She swept in. "Franny told me a little about the situation. I think it's absurd."

"Ms. Hurley," Principal Harrow said. He was beginning to look a little gray.

"Franny's article was outspoken and opinionated and, yes, in some ways it was shocking. But I think it belonged in the paper, even if some students took a sneaky way to get it in there. It was an article that needed to be printed. We should respect their understanding of that—more, I would argue, than the arbitrary whims of another teenager, even if the other student does happen to be editor."

Principal Harrow pursed his lips.

"Do you know how hard Franny worked on that article?" Zooey said. "Every night, for two weeks, she was calling people or sitting in front of her computer."

"If people do whatever they want, why bother having an editor?" River shot back.

"Don't you mean, 'Why bother having a *censor*?'" Carter threw in.

I sat back and listened to them stew.

"I will shut down the paper rather than have this squabbling continue!" Principal Harrow fumed.

"Oh, please, El Jefe!" Zooey said. I smashed my lips together to keep from laughing. All this time I thought Zooey and I were so different, but it turned out she had the exact same mouth-shutting issues as I did.

"Hey!" I cut in, surprised by my own vehemence. "Can I talk for a second? I don't care about who should or shouldn't have done what. I just care that a lot of people thought my article was cool and I want to write more like it. Please don't shut down the paper; is there a way to figure out how to make it work so I can write more and we can do the things newspapers are supposed to do?" I realized everyone was looking at me like I had just descended from the mother ship. "What?" I said.

"It's just . . ." River paused, looking at me curiously. "You're usually not so definite, Franny. This whole semester, you've been so tongue-tied, I could never have seen you as a columnist." He kept his eyes glued on my face. "I bet you would be good at it."

Well, I had fallen down a rabbit hole. It could happen to anyone.

"I can't believe it's taken you *this* long to realize that," I answered River. "I'm glad you finally see something in me and my writing. But Carter got it from the first time we started talking. That matters so much more." I looked at Principal Harrow. "So. Is there a way to work this out?"

chapter 34

When we finally emerged from Principal Harrow's office, Brianna was waiting for us, pouting her freshly glossed lips and readjusting her uniform skirt. As she walked up to River, her fingers trailed across his knapsack and up his arm, squeezing his shoulder. He caught her hand and pulled her in toward him.

And, then, they began necking.

If the words *good grief* floated through my head one more time, I would officially be Charlie Brown.

"Let's get out of here," Zooey said loudly. In another moment, steam was going to start puffing from her ears.

"Gladly," I answered. I grinned at her and Carter. "Let's go celebrate." Then, because two (OK, four) could play that game, I reached down and took Carter's hand in mine.

"I ought to do this hell-raising thing every week," he said, smiling back at me.

"It honestly might not have worked out so well without Ms. Hurley," I said, glancing behind me. "She was really cool about the whole thing."

"We probably should have had a faculty adviser long before now, anyway," Carter agreed. "Even if Ms. Hurley does have to approve every single layout before it goes to the printer, I bet she'll be reasonable."

River and Brianna managed detach their lips from each other long enough to flounce in front of us. Probably, he wasn't really a villain. He was probably just a harmless but extreme flirt.

"I can't believe how well it worked out," I said. "I mean, none of us got in trouble, and . . . you know."

"You're now a columnist," Carter filled in.

Columnist. The weirdest part was that I hadn't known how much I wanted it until I was sitting in Principal Harrow's office and realized it might never happen. Happily, I slung one arm gently around Zooey's crutch and the other around Carter's neck, and we wandered out of the school.

Much later that night, after we had gotten home and I'd updated Rhia and had my first official writer's block brainstorming topics for next week's column, I decided Zooey and I still had unfinished business.

"Hi," I said, dropping into her room after a quick knock. "I have to ask you something."

She looked up from the book she was reading and made an mm-hmming sound.

"Why'd you come to my school today?"

"I told you, I wanted to apologize to Principal Harrow."

Last spring, Zooey puked all over the model of Versailles that my history group had spent three weeks making for our team project. We had put tiny bonsai trees in the gardens and actual mirrors in the Hall of Mirrors. Then we had to start it all over again the day before it was due.

No apology. Zooey just claimed her stomach had a mind of its own.

"Why do I not entirely believe you?" I asked.

Zooey sat up. "Can I trust you with something? You wouldn't tell anyone?"

"Well, I only take plastic for bribes these days." I giggled.

Zooey, looking serious, passed over a thick sheaf of official-looking papers and sign-here flags. I studied it.

"It's a ballet contract," she said. "To join the company as a professional dancer next year. You know, when I get done with physical therapy."

"Huh," I said aloud. "I thought that was a given."

She shook her head. "They're not sure I'm ready. They're only giving me a chance because Arturo Peretti is moving to New York permanently to choreograph for the company and he likes me." She giggled. "Which is insane, because he's Arturo Peretti and I'm just, you know . . ." She trailed off.

"Well, congrats," I offered.

Zooey sat up and tugged her blue comforter around her shoulders, like a shawl. "Except I don't know that I want to do it," she said quietly.

"What?"

"It's like I told you; maybe I missed out on a lot by being on the twenty-four–seven ballet track. So I had this bizarre idea that maybe before I actually put my name on the dotted line, I should ask Principal Harrow about going to school for a little while, until my leg healed. Just so I would know what I was missing."

"Wow, you've really changed," I said slowly.

"I could be anything," she said. "I never realized it. I could do whatever I want."

"I can't believe you're not going to sign the contract," I blurted. "I thought that *was* what you wanted."

Zooey looked up at the ceiling. "Did you notice that Principal Harrow has the biggest mole on the planet? It's like a chocolate chip is welded behind his ear."

"How can you have a crisis over ballet?" I asked.

Zooey shrugged.

"That's like Smurfette having a crisis whether or not to be blue," I added.

"Well, being blue totally limits your fashion choices." Zooey kicked her leg in the cast upward.

"I *think* I'll sign. I just . . ." She trailed off.

"You should do it. You should try school just until you join the company," I said.

"What if I don't want to join then?"

Good question. "Then you'll know you're not meant to be a ballerina. How long do you have before you have to let them know?"

"Sooner is better, but I think before they start casting in the spring."

"That's *months* away," I said. "Come to school. It would be kind of fun to have you there."

"I'll probably fail out; it's been forever since I've been in a real school."

"Come," I repeated. "You can get in another food fight."

Zooey gave me a scathing look. "Oh, ha."

chapter 35

Zooey wasn't the only one having eureka moments. Having finally decided that our apartment was not exactly in the *House Beautiful* mode, Dad had opened his own eyes enough to hire a cleaning service. Somehow, the fridge also got cleaned and restocked, and vases of tulips (Mom's favorite flower) were scattered around. Mom, who was due in the Tuesday before Thanksgiving, might actually be fooled into thinking we hadn't been living like cave rats this whole time.

The day she got in also happened to be production day for the paper. Even though River was jerkily pretending he had somehow *discovered* me, Carter had somehow taken on this rebel-leader status on staff, and our new issue felt edgier and more opinionated. Anyway, given my newly minted columnist status, I felt it might be poor form to skip out before production was over, so I just left a note at home that I'd be there as soon as I could. The newspaper room had rotten cell reception, which meant I had a slew of messages by the time I left school: Mom had made it home.

Home. As in, she was sitting in our freshly (and, let's face it, fakely) cleaned living room at this very second. I knew that I should probably be walking as fast as I could, but for some reason my feet were barely moving, like a wind-up toy just before it fell over. It was almost like I was incapable of going faster.

"Hello?" I said, letting myself into the apartment. I could hear loud talking coming from the living room. "Helll-ooo," I called again.

"Franny!" Mom was in the hallway in a flash. "Oh, Franny!" I felt her arms go around me, holding a little too tightly. Tears sprang into my eyes. I was going to hate myself if I went all after-school special and actually started bawling, so I pulled away.

"Oh, I missed you," she said, reaching out a hand to smooth my hair.

"Really?" I asked.

"Of course! What do you mean, 'really'?" She shook her head at me, moving her hand down my hair to rest on my shoulder. Her hair was longer than it had been, and she had a small diamond chip resting on the side of her right nostril.

"You got your nose pierced?" I asked incredulously.

Once again, my parents were taking long, greedy guzzles from the Fountain of Inappropriate Youth.

She made a face. "Well, it seemed like a good idea at the time."

"Let me guess," I broke in. "*Everyone* was doing it? And then they all decided to jump off a cliff? And you jumped too?"

She laughed. "I *have* missed you."

I shuffled back and forth, not sure of what else to say. "So, do you have to stick your finger up your nose to get it in and out?" I attempted.

"Changing the topic now," Dad broke in, coming to stand next to Mom. He had on a very, very old NYU sweatshirt that I hadn't seen him wear in a long time and looked about as hipster as a ball of yarn.

"If you got your nose pierced, is it OK if I get a real tattoo?" I asked. "Not just a henna one?"

Dad shrugged lazily. "I'd say it depends on what you want. I'd say no winged hearts, no boys' names, and no dragons." He frowned. "And no Celtic symbols. They're past their due date."

Amish. Maybe they would care if I became Amish.

We ended up making a big vat of spaghetti for dinner, and sat around the table having a spaghetti-slurping contest. Mom had brought us a lot of presents, baskets and jewelry and all, and she had stories about all the different anthropologists living in the camp. It's strange; I never really thought of my mom as funny, but for some reason, I couldn't stop laughing.

I wished it didn't feel so nice to have her home.

The next night, we started getting ready for Thanksgiving, even dragging out the pinecone turkeys Zooey and I had made back in elementary school. They were so old and brittle by now that some of the feathers were falling off. I picked them up. Mine was a bit haphazard, the head cut unevenly out of construction paper with a crookedly attached gullet and a gaping, open beak. Zooey's was crumbling from age (pinecones not being the sort of things one typically saves as family heirlooms), but I could tell how perfectly aligned everything must have been when she first made it. Not a glue bubble or sloppy scissors mark in sight. How very Zooey.

I put the turkeys back down on the table between the candlesticks and wandered into the kitchen. Mom was vigorously rolling out a piecrust. I watched her for a moment.

"Can I do that?" I asked.

She looked up. "Sure." She handed the rolling pin over and showed me how to roll in a V-shape until the crust was just a little thinner than the top of my cell phone. "This is the tricky part. We fold it into quarters," she said, the crust sticking to itself and cracking a little, "and then unfold it into the pan." As she did, the crust tore jaggedly.

"Crudmonster," she muttered. "I always do that." She began patching the crust together with water and little scraps of extra crust, muttering occasional obscenities as she worked. "My mom taught me how to make a piecrust when I was about your age," she said, looking over at me. "She'd just been diagnosed with cancer and we didn't really know what it meant, but there was no way she was going to leave the earth unless her daughter could make a piecrust."

I shifted awkwardly. My grandma died when my mom was in her first year of college. We talked about our belly button lint more than we talked about her.

"The only reason I ever make pies is because I know it was important to her that I be able to do it," Mom continued. She started spooning apple filling in. "Why don't you take over?"

I took the bowl from her. "I tried to cook dinner once," I said. "It was a catastrophe."

"Dad told me," she said.

"Well, I thought I needed to," I said awkwardly. *Since there was no other way we were going to get food because you were off continent-hopping . . .*

I didn't say the last part aloud, but I think Mom maybe got the point because she didn't say anything else, just started showing me how to cut the lattice for the top. While I was folding it into the pattern, she made a small motion like she was going to touch my head but then dropped her hand.

"You shouldn't feel you have to take my place," she said.

There were about a hundred million things I'd rather do than get into this conversation with my mother.

"Ummm," I said eloquently.

"Or that you're the one who needs to take care of everything."

"Ummm."

"Or that I wouldn't love to be here if I could."

All of a sudden, I was done ummm-ing.

"You don't know *anything* that went on while you were away, do you?" I said. "How could you just sail out of here and leave us like that? And Dad, he's been lonely, and I'm practically failing half my classes and Zooey's hurt and it's like you don't know and you don't care to know because you're all so busy with your new life studying these fascinating other families. I hate that you left us." All of a sudden, something in me snapped. I picked up the pie and threw it onto the floor. "I hate *you*!"

Then, because I was suddenly too exhausted to do anything else, I sank onto the kitchen floor and sat there, very shaky. I couldn't remember ever doing anything so completely bratty in my entire life. What was wrong with me?

Mom knelt and brushed some apples and crusts away. "Can I sit here?" she asked.

"I said I hated you."

"I heard," she said softly, settling onto the floor.

"You're always telling me I should express myself. Aren't you glad I finally listened?" I said, sniffing in my tears as best I could.

"Overjoyed."

I'd spent so much time over the past few months wanting my mom (or, more accurately, pretending that I *didn't* want her), and now that she was here, I freaked on her. Grand. I wouldn't blame her if she decided to stay on another continent permanently.

"I'm sorry," she said at last. "You're right."

I shook my head. "No, I'm not. I shouldn't have said any of that." Just once, I would like to go through an entire day without doing something to appall myself.

"You're right, though, Franny." She bit her lip. "I'm not glad you felt you needed to say it, but I am glad you felt you *could* say it. Does that make sense?"

"No."

"I would be lying if I said that the past few months haven't been life-changing for me. They have been . . ." She stopped. "Astonishing."

How delightful for her.

"And I feel guilty about that," she added. "I didn't think it would be such a big deal to be back in the field."

"Are you coming home ever?" I asked bitterly.

Mom looked like I'd slapped her. "Oh, honey, of course I'm coming home."

"Are you *sure*?"

Mom hugged me. Hard. I tried to wriggle away and she just closed her arms tighter. "Yes, I'm sure."

"Are you learning all sorts of new-age, touchy-feely crap in Kenya?" I muttered.

She laughed and let go. "I'm coming home in the spring, the same as we always planned." She tilted her head to the side. "Can we agree to something? I'll call more and you do the same, especially if you're feeling overwhelmed?"

"We can try that."

"Now, dare I ask, are you really failing half your classes?"

"Well, I think I might get some extra credit," I said aloud. "But I might not expect the greatest grades from me this term."

"Gotcha," Mom said. Then, "Am I going to meet Carter while I'm here?"

I nodded. "If you want."

"I do."

"He's kind of awesome."

"Only 'kind of' awesome?"

"Very awesome," I clarified. I looked at the floor around us, with pie chunks of apple and crust spewed everywhere. "I'm sorry about the pie. I can't believe I did that."

"We'll make another." Mom stood up and looked at me speculatively. "Is it possible you grew when I was away?"

"I hope so!" I had long since relinquished hope of being

model-tall. On the other hand, if I actually managed to hit five feet, I could die tomorrow. We could put "A great miracle happened here" on the grave.

"You just look so much bigger and older to me," Mom said, pulling out the tape measure.

"I believe the word you want is *statuesque*," I said, standing as straight as I could.

"Four feet, ten," Mom read.

Aw, crap. Exactly the same as I'd been at my last check.

Well, you couldn't win them all. And, anyway, last I'd heard, good things came in small packages.

chapter 36

Probably, someday, they will discover that turkey has magical powers. Then the Red Cross can start airlifting it over the world. By the end of Mom's visit, and a lot of Thanksgiving leftovers, I felt amazingly cheerful—better than I had in months.

"Promise me you'll write?" she said, hugging me good-bye at the airport.

I nodded, watching as she rolled her big suitcase through the sliding doors. There was a small lump in my throat. I swallowed, hard.

"You want to go back to the city?" the cabdriver said. "I can take you back to where I picked you up."

"Could you take me to Lincoln Center instead?"

"Lincoln Center? Sure. You going to see something?"

"Romeo and Juliet." Zooey had said I didn't need to go to opening night with her, but I kind of wanted to anyway. I didn't trust the ballet people to be civil.

"Posters for that show are everywhere," he said.

"Everywhere," I agreed, checking my watch. We wouldn't be back into the city for a while. Settling into the backseat, I pulled out the copy of *Franny and Zooey* I'd tucked into my bag. I figured I had to start it sometime.

We ended up hitting a lot of traffic, so I didn't get to the theater until after the performance had started. Since they wouldn't let me go to my seat in the middle of the show, I sat in the lobby, still reading, until crowds started filtering out for intermission. It took a long time for Zooey to get there. At last she crutched out, orbited by a mob of lithely tall and very wrinkled people.

"It should have been you," one of them cried, leaning over to knock on Zooey's cast as though it were wood.

"You know, she's been offered a spot in the company," another woman chimed in. "Arturo insisted."

Zooey smiled modestly. Then she saw me waving. "Franny!" she squealed. I made my way through the crowd to stand beside her and Dad. "This is my sister, Franny," she explained. "You've met her."

As usual, I could feel the scrutiny of the ballet eyes scanning up and down my body. I felt my spine straighten itself inadvertently.

"So, Franny," one of the women asked, chewing slightly on the slash of pink lipstick across her mouth. I flinched, knowing what was coming. "What kind of dance do you do?"

"I'm not a dancer." For some reason, it felt easier to say tonight.

"Hmmm," the woman mused politely. "But your joints look like they could handle it."

"She does have her sister's build," another said, fingering my shoulder.

"It's probably too late for her." A third looked at me shrewdly. "You've *never* trained?"

"I'm not interested." I had always assumed the ballet scrutiny was because I didn't look like a dancer. But maybe I'd been wrong.

"Franny's going to be a journalist," Zooey broke in. "And she's my best friend."

The ballet women suddenly began cooing. "That's so *sweet*," one of them said.

"Have you read *Franny and Zooey*?" another asked.

"Actually"—I held it up—"I just started it."

"You did?" Zooey asked.

"I'm loving it so far," I said honestly. "You have to read it, too."

"Of course," Zooey said. "Hey, you have somewhere else to be, don't you, Franny?"

Rhia and I *had* talked about getting together. But I told her I'd probably be at *Romeo and Juliet* all night.

"Do you mind?" I asked.

"I'll walk you out," Zooey said. Slowly, we made our way through the crowds, into the plaza outside the theater. There was a Christmas tree already up, twinkling with lights.

"How'd you know I had to be someplace else?" I asked. "I didn't tell you."

She shrugged. "Lucky guess."

"How's Dominique as Juliet?"

"Sadly, she's very good. But I think I want to audition for a new role for next year, as soon as I get the cast off. It's Cinderella."

Once upon a time, I might have made jokes about Zooey and wicked stepsisters. "You said I was your best friend in there?" I said questioningly. More and more, I'd been thinking of her as my best friend also.

"So I got a little mushy." She shrugged. "You have lots of friends. I have . . . you. And I'm working on finding some more." She stared at the plaza. There were a few people milling around, but for the most part, we were the only ones there. "Do you think I can do a jeté?" she asked suddenly.

"A what?"

"I bet I can. I bet my leg is strong enough."

"What are you doing?" I gasped as she rose onto her toes.

She took three small steps forward, then jumped, cast and all, into the air, her legs cleaving apart into a perfect line.

"Zooey!" I shrieked. "Don't do that!"

"Why not?" Her laughter floated back to me. "I can balance OK."

"Because you'll hurt yourself again."

"Then you try it."

"I'm not a dancer."

"I know. Just try it. Just this once."

I sighed. "You're silly."

"Before you leave, just do it."

"Zooey."

"Franny," she said in the exact same tone of voice. "What are you waiting for?"

"I'm really leaving after this," I promised.

"Fine."

I took a deep breath and stared at the plaza. Then, running as fast as I could, I jumped into the empty space ahead.

acknowledgments

Writing this book—while finishing a Ph.D. and moving cross-country—required a superhuman level of support and patience from those around me. Many thanks go out to my agent, Jenny Bent, and editor, Hilary Teeman. In addition, I'd like to thank Jill and Lloyd Lewis, Michael and Camille Mendle, Chris and Nicky Mendle, Ann Frosch, Jonathan Cobb, Alessia Donati, Nicole Bond, Ben Strong, Lisa Halliday, Anna Tush, Jeanine Stefanucci, and Paige Harden, all of whom have been integral sources of support and, even on the grumpiest days, have made me laugh.